Killing the Emperors

Books by Ruth Dudley Edwards

The Robert Amiss Mysteries
Clubbed to Death
The English School of Murder
The St. Valentine's Day Murders
Corridors of Death

The Jack Troutbeck/Robert Amiss Mysteries
Carnage on the Committee
The Anglo-Irish Murders
Publish and Be Murdered
Murder in a Cathedral
Ten Lords A-Leaping
Matricide at St. Martha's
Murdering Americans
Killing the Emperors

Nonfiction
Newspapermen: Hugh Cudlipp, Cecil Harmsworth
King and the Glory Days of Fleet Street
The Faithful Tribe: An Intimate Portrait of the Loyal Institutions
True Brits: Inside the Foreign Office
The Best of Bagehot
The Pursuit of Reason: The Economist 1843–1993
Victor Gollancz: A Biography
Harold MacMillan: A Life in Pictures
James Connolly
Patrick Pearse: The Triumph of Failure
An Atlas of Irish History
Aftermath: The Omagh Bombing
and the Families' Pursuit of Justice

Killing the Emperors

A Jack Troutbeck/ Robert Amiss Mystery

Ruth Dudley Edwards

Poisoned Pen Press

Library of Congress Catalog Card Number: 2010937029

ISBN: 9781590586389   Hardcover
        9781464200496   Trade Paperback

Poisoned Pen Press
6962 E. First Ave., Ste. 103
Scottsdale, AZ 85251
www.poisonedpenpress.com
info@poisonedpenpress.com

Printed in the United States of America

To Robert, friend and ally,
who passed on to me the excellent advice that—
since there's usually nothing to laugh at—
one should learn to laugh at nothing

'Nothing that you will learn in the course of your studies will be of the slightest possible use to you in after life—save only this—that if you work hard and intelligently you should be able to detect *when a man is talking rot*, and that, in my view, is the main, if not the sole, purpose of education.'

—John Alexander Smith,
Waynflete Professor of Moral and Metaphysical Philosophy,
Oxford, 1914

Dramatis personae

I've indicated old friends and in which book and number in the series they first appeared: 1 *Corridors of Death* (*CoD*); 2 *The St. Valentine's Day Murders* (*TSVDM*); 3 *The English School of Murder (TESoM)*; 5 *Matricide at St. Martha's* (MaSM); 10 *Carnage on the Committee* (*CotC*)

Robert Amiss, ex-civil servant and holder of a variety of jobs, who was the main character in this series until in *MaSM* Troutbeck turned him into a sidekick (*CoD*)

Charlie Briggs, hedge-fundie with more money than sense

Sarah Byrne, competent constable

Myles Cavendish, ex-SAS (Special Air Service of the British Army), Baroness Troutbeck's favourite and occasionally live-in lover (*MaSM*)

Martin Conroy, employed by Inland Revenue, ex-SAS reserve

Mary Lou Dinsmore, African American ex-lover of Troutbeck, academic-turned-BBC-arts-presenter, now married to Ellis Pooley (*MaSM*)

Adam Eichberg, celebrity auctioneer

Sir Henry Fortune, careerist curator and senior lover of Jason Pringle

Chester Herblock, opportunistic American art consultant

Anastasia Holliday, Australian performance artist on the make

Horace, currently resting parrot (*CotC*)

Marilyn Falucci Lamont, billionairess American socialite and art collector

Jim Milton, Commander at Scotland Yard, who often has a tough time; long-time friend of Amiss' (*CoD*)

Vernon Morrison, lazy constable

Plutarch, horrible cat (*TESoM*)

Ellis Pooley, earnest Old Etonian Detective Inspector, right-hand man of Jim Milton, close friend of Amiss and husband of Mary Lou Dinsmore (*TSVDM*)

Jason Pringle, amoral art dealer and senior lover of Sir Henry Fortune

Mike Rogers, ex-SAS colleague of Myles Cavendish

Rachel Simon, Amiss' on-off girlfriend and now wife; diplomat-turned-teacher (*TSVDM*)

Oleg Sarkovsky, dodgy Russian oligarch obsessed with status

Sir Nicholas Serota, Director of the Tate galleries and sadly—like all the artists in this book other than Holliday—not a figment of my imagination

Jake Thorogood, corrupted art critic

Baroness Ida 'Jack' Troutbeck, Mistress of St. Martha's, self-indulgent, happy reactionary (*MaSM*)

Gavin Truss, 'if-you-think-it's-art-it's-art' head of an art college

Hortense Wilde, priggish ideological art historian

Anyone called Zeka—nasty Albanian contract killers

"The Emperor's New Clothes"

by Hans Christian Andersen

Once upon a time there lived a vain emperor who was obsessed with dressing elegantly and showing his clothes off to his people.

Word of his refined habits spread over his kingdom and attracted two scoundrels to the palace. 'We are two very good tailors,' they said, 'and after many years of research we can weave a cloth so light and fine that it looks invisible to anyone who is too stupid and incompetent to appreciate its quality.'

The chief of the guards sent for the court chamberlain, who notified the prime minister, who ran to the emperor with the incredible news. The emperor received the scoundrels, who told him that the cloth would not only be invisible, but would be woven in wonderful colours and patterns created especially for him. Delighted to know that as well as having an extraordinary suit, he would discover which of his subjects were ignorant and incompetent, he gave them a bag of gold and had them equipped with a loom, silk, and gold thread. After a few days he called the old and wise prime minister, revered for his common sense, and instructed him to find out how the work was proceeding.

"We're almost finished, but we need a lot more gold thread," the scoundrels told the prime minister. 'Here, Excellency! Admire the colours, feel the softness!' The old man bent over the loom and tried to see the fabric that was not there and felt cold sweat on his forehead.

"I can't see anything," he thought. "If I see nothing, that means I'm stupid or incompetent and I'll be fired.' So he praised the fabric and reported favourably to the emperor.

When the scoundrels met the emperor to measure him for his suit, they showed him the imaginary fabric. 'Look at the colours and feel how fine it is.' Of course the emperor did not see any colours and could not feel any cloth between his fingers and he almost panicked. But when he realized that no one could know that he couldn't see the fabric and realise he was stupid and incompetent, he recovered.

Finally, the scoundrels brought him the invisible suit. He took off his clothes, put it on and looked in a mirror. The Emperor was embarrassed but since none of his bystanders were, he felt relieved. 'Yes, this is beautiful and it looks very good on me,' he said.

'Your Majesty,' requested the prime minister, 'the people have heard about this extraordinary fabric and want to see you in your new suit.' The emperor was doubtful, but then he realised that only the ignorant and incompetent would realise he was naked.

The ceremonial parade was formed. A group of dignitaries walked at the very front of the procession and anxiously scrutinized the faces of the people in the street. All the people had gathered in the main square, pushing and shoving to get a better look. Applause welcomed the regal procession. Worried that they couldn't see the clothes, and fearful of admitting their stupidity and incompetence, the crowd began to make laudatory comments. 'Look at the emperor's new clothes. They're beautiful!' 'What a marvellous train.' 'And the colours! The colours of that beautiful fabric! I've never seen anything like it in my life!'

However, a child, who had no job to protect and could see only what his eyes showed him, ran up to the carriage and cried, 'The emperor hasn't anything on.'.

'Fool!' his father shouted, running after him. 'Don't talk nonsense!' He grabbed his child and hustled him away. But the boy's remark, which had been heard by the bystanders, was repeated over and over again until everyone cried: 'The boy is right! The emperor is naked! It's true!'

The emperor could not admit that he knew the people were right and thought it better to maintain the illusion that anyone who couldn't see his clothes was either stupid or incompetent. And he walked more proudly than ever, with his noblemen holding high the train that wasn't there at all.

Prologue

March 2012

'Yes, Sarge. Right away, Sarge,' said Constable Vernon Morrison. He switched off his radio crossly and gave it a two-fingered salute. 'More bollocks,' he said to Constable Sarah Byrne. 'Now he says we're to do a detour via the South Bank to see if any troublesome lowlifes need picking up. And we're to check anywhere they might be hiding and up to no good.' His fingers went up again. 'Well, I bloody don't want to. And I won't. We've patrolled up and down and around every blasted road within a radius of half-a-mile of effin' Waterloo Station till my legs are dropping off. I'm totally knackered.'

'But, Vernon…'

'Don't you "but Vernon" me. I'm freezin'. I don't need no stroll by the effin' river; I need a sausage sandwich and a mug of tea.'

He made a poor shot at mimicking a pedantic voice: '"The reputation of London is at stake, Morrison! We cannot have tourists bothered by aggressive beggars, Morrison! Move them on, Morrison! Move them on!" What planet's he on? What tourists in their right minds are going to be hangin' round by the river this time of night in this weather?'

Byrne adopted the cheery tone that usually worked when her three-year-old was whining. 'Tell you what, Vernon, why don't we head for that cab shelter near the Embankment? They'll have good sausages. And if we get there via the South Bank, everyone will be happy. It won't take any longer to get there that way and we won't have to fib to Sarge.'

This had the hoped-for magical effect. 'You're right, Sarah. Those boys do a good sausage sandwich. OK, we can go that route, but you need to know I'm not goin' into any holes and corners. There's more of them around here than the Sarge has braincells. And this time of night, they'll be pongin' to high heaven.'

Cleverer, more ambitious and more conscientious than her older colleague, Byrne had brought humouring him to a fine art. Within a couple of minutes Morrison was plodding along uncomplainingly by her side on the way to the South Bank while deep in reminiscences about how he had built up the model railway that so annoyed his wife. He was so interested in what he was saying that he made no protest when she occasionally shone her torch into the shadows.

As they reached the side of the National Theatre, a chill wind dissipated his good humour. 'Why are we botherin', Sarah? All decent people will have gone home by now. Who cares what's happenin' in the dark corners? The only ones there will be the pissers, the pissed, and the passed out.' He snorted appreciatively at his wit. 'Come on. Speed up and head for Embankment Bridge.'

Not for the first time, Sarah wondered what use this fat slob was to anyone and why he thought the tax payer should subsidise his laziness. But he was the experienced officer and she was the rookie and she realised she could no longer keep him on the path of duty even if she used the desperate expedient of asking him if he was planning to buy any more rolling stock in the near future. Morrison quickened his pace as they swung into the South Bank. They reached the undercroft where skateboarders leaped and twisted and skidded and fell off all day and she flashed her torch.

'There's no one there, Sarah. Even those nutters don't risk life and limb here in the middle of a winter night.'

'I thought I heard someone calling.'

'I bloody didn't. And even if I did, I wouldn't care. Come on. My sausages call.' Looking back guiltily, she saw a dishevelled figure emerging from the gloom and beckoning vigorously. 'Hang on, Vernon. There's a bloke wants a word.' She stood her ground and Morrison stopped reluctantly.

'Bloody wino,' he said, as the gaunt, bearded man caught up with them.

He looked at Morrison resentfully. 'I may be a bloody wino,' he said, in an accent more educated that Morrison's, 'but I'm not blind. And I'm not stupid. There's someone hanging in there and you should be seeing if you can save him.'

'Oh, for fuck's sake! You're seein' things.' Morrison adopted his most patronising tone. 'It may have escaped you—it being dark and all—and you havin' had a few, if the smell of whisky is anything to go by—but that whole underground bit is covered from top to bottom with graffiti of people doin' all sorts of things. Probably includin' hanging. Them sort of images are all the rage these days. It's called modern art.'

'I'm not seeing things. Someone's hanging in the corner at the back on the left. He's all in black so I wouldn't have noticed him only it was the best place to sleep. And he's hanging from too far up for me to reach.'

'You'd better be right about this,' said Morrison. 'Wouldn't do you no good to waste police time.'

'What's your name, sir?' asked Byrne, to Morrison's disgust.

'George. Glad to see someone with manners.'

'Could you show us, please?' The undercroft was quite well lit, but the corner at which George pointed was very dark and she needed her torch. A grumbling 'it stinks' indicated that Morrison was following. George stopped, she followed the line of his pointing finger and shone the light up a wall at something long, dangling, and black. A snort came from behind. 'You know what that is?' said Morrison. 'That's another one of them so-called graffiti-paintings by that vandal Banksy. You see them black balloons? He's famous for balloons.'

As the beam of Byrne's torch moved up and down, Morrison shouted triumphantly, 'Look at that placard. I'm right. It even says "Banksy." In big letters.'

Uncertainly, Sarah went up close to the figure and touched it. Feeling cloth, she tugged, and the light fabric tumbled to the ground. 'Vernon, you dickhead,' she yelled. 'I don't care if it says 'Leonardo da fucking Vinci' on it. It's a real man with a noose around his neck. Don't you think we should find out if he's dead?'

Chapter One

January 2012

'I used to want to kill the talentless so-called artists,' said Baroness Troutbeck, 'but now I want instead to fill the tumbrils with the critics, the dealers, the curators, and all the rest of the charlatans and dunderheads peddling trash in the name of contemporary art.'

She paused for a moment, tugged absent-mindedly on the massive rope of jet that stood out starkly against her voluminous red kaftan, reached for her glass, and had another sip. 'Not forgetting, of course, all those who wrecked the art colleges and chucked out into the world generations proud to be untutored and unskilled. The gullible little wretches were convinced that you could be an artist without being able to paint, draw, or sculpt. Or for that matter know anything at all about painting, drawing, or sculpture. Or beauty.'

She took another sip, nodded approvingly, settled herself more comfortably in her vast green leather armchair and beamed at her friends. 'These martinis really are excellent, don't you think? Sometimes it's a bit of a chore being chairman of ffeatherstonehaugh's,[1] but if it means you have somewhere you can rely on getting decent food and drink it's worth putting in the effort.'

---

1   For the story set in the ffeatherstonehaugh's gentlemen's club, see *Clubbed to Death*

'I still prefer vodka martinis, Jack,' said Mary Lou Denslow.

'You really must grow out of your filthy American habits, Mary Lou. Vodka is for people without taste buds. Which of course sadly all Americans are. Martinis are to gin as Roman Catholicism is to the pope.' She frowned. 'Well, to Roman Catholic popes, that is. These days there's no guarantee that a pope will necessarily be a Catholic. I expect that in the interests of inclusiveness there will be a call for the next one to be a Wiccan single lesbian mother on benefits. Perhaps I should offer myself as a compromise candidate.' She took yet another sip, smacked her lips appreciatively, and smiled seraphically. 'Now apropos the gin, it's absolutely vital that you chose either....'

'Oh, shut up, Jack,' said Mary Lou. 'Get back to business. Why are you allowing the artists to live? What happened to your plan to have Damien Hirst pickled in formaldehyde and called *The Physical Impossibility of Producing Art if You've No Fucking Talent?*'

'I dithered a bit about this. I was tempted by the alternative of having him cut in half, dangling the bits from a gibbet, and calling the result *Hanged for a Calf?*'

Ellis Pooley raised an enquiring eyebrow. 'You're losing me, Jack. I've heard of Damien Hirst and know he made money out of a dead shark, but that's about it. Where does a calf come into it?'

'What sheltered lives you must lead at Scotland Yard.'

'For God's sake, Ellis,' broke in Robert Amiss. 'How can you be married to Mary Lou...'

'The thinking man's crumpet,' beamed the baroness.

'Stop stealing old jokes, Jack,' said Mary Lou. 'That one dates from the seventies.'

'The old ones are the best, Mary Lou. Like Joan Bakewell, the prototype! Dreadful leftie and had an affair with that ghastly pseud Harold Pinter, but so very fanciable. Even now.'

'As I was saying,' said Amiss, 'how, Ellis, can you be married to the culture industry's iconic broadcaster and not know anything about art?'

'I know quite a bit about art,' said Pooley indignantly. 'Decent art, that is. I just ignore most modern art because I'm too busy to waste my time looking at rubbish.'

'Can't argue with that,' said the baroness. 'Mary Lou, you're paid to comment on crap. Explain Hirst to your husband.'

Mary Lou sighed. 'If I must. Ellis, you know about the YBAs.'

'No.'

'Oh, stop it, Ellis,' said Amiss. 'I know you're a fogey but now you're sounding like an octogenarian judge.'

Mary Lou patted her husband's hand. 'The Young British Artists, hon. Hirst and Tracey Emin and so on. The ones who made BritArt big business over the last couple of decades.'

'Oh, them! Yes, of course. Emin's that dreadful woman who made a fortune from her filthy bed.'

'That's the one, darling. Complete with empty vodka bottles, condoms, tampons, and much else you'd rather not think about before dinner.'

'Or even afterwards,' said Pooley.

'The egregious Tracey specialises in what you might call the cartography of the knicker stain,' said the baroness grimly. 'They were presenting that sort of trash as art in a hundred art colleges years ago, but Emin was so noisy and shameless she attracted attention. And, of course, the vandals of the art world took her up. They like them loud and disgusting. It's *épater les bourgeois* all over again. Only this time it's the smug, well-heeled, liberal establishment doing the épatering.'

'Emin's a fame whore, Ellis,' said Mary Lou patiently. 'And very successful at it. She sells her horrid pointless installations and crude drawings by providing a complementary narrative of confessional and self-revelatory bullshit. She's also been smart about becoming pals with existing celebrities, and aspiring celebrities flock to be photographed with her. She became a Conservative supporter just as it appeared inevitable they'd be getting into government and the prime minister is so keen to seem cool that he declared himself a fan and asked her to provide Number 10, Downing Street, with an artwork to give it a bit of "edge."'

Pooley groaned.

'I read about that,' said Amiss. 'A neon sign flashing *More Passion* in scruffy handwriting, wasn't it?'

'Yep.'

'I'd have preferred it if it said *Smaller Government*,' said the baroness gloomily. 'Or *Lower Taxes*. Or *Fiscal Continence*. Or *Why don't you meddling little Napoleons just piss off and leave me alone?*'

Mary Lou laughed. 'You probably have the same politics as she does. These days she seems passionate mostly about tax rates. She threatened to leave the country when the fifty percent higher rate came in.'

There was a long sigh from Pooley. He leaned forward and picked up his glass. 'It's enough to drive even me to drink. Don't tell me *More Passion* was paid for from our taxes?'

'No, hon. It was a gift that's been arbitrarily valued by the media at a quarter of a million, thus enabling artistic luvvies to cry that Tracey is a true patriot. Mind you, she produces plenty of neon signs, and having one in a prominent position in Number 10 should at least treble their value. Probably helped her become Professor of Drawing at the Royal Academy.'

'Can she draw?' asked a depressed Pooley.

'A bit. Not well. It doesn't matter. She's on her way to becoming Dame Tracey. Or even Lady Emin.'

The baroness winced. 'We've already got enough vulgarians in the Lords. Mind you, I suppose she deserves credit for exercising some decorum in her Downing Street choice. I remember two of her earlier neons that asked respectively *Is Anal Sex Legal?* and *Is Legal Sex Anal?* Now those would certainly have been edgy, especially when the PM was entertaining ayatollahs.'

She sighed. 'Mind you, they didn't even have the virtue of originality. In the seventies, another pretentious but more talented git called Bruce Nauman produced a neon light that said *Run From Fear/Fun From Rear*. However, I digress. Let's get back to Hirst, who was the leader of that particular artistic pack. He knew how to fleece credulous halfwits. He first hit the headlines when his piece involving maggots and flies feeding off the head of a dead cow wowed Charles Saatchi.'

'I know about Saatchi too,' said Pooley. 'A plutocratic adman who made another big fortune out of dreadful art.'

'He's married to Nigella Lawson,' said the baroness. 'Yum, yum. That's Nigella. Not her food.' She paused. 'Well, the food's not bad, but compared to Nigella's sumptuous…'

'Stop drooling, Jack,' said Mary Lou. 'Saatchi offered Hirst a £50,000 commission to do whatever he darned well liked and the result was a shark in formaldehyde in a giant glass tank (or vitrine, as the cognoscenti call it) called *The Physical Impossibility of Death in the Mind of Someone Living*.'

'Hence my *The Physical Impossibility of Producing Art if You've No Fucking Talent*,' beamed the baroness. 'But tell Ellis what happened to the unfortunate shark.'

'It rotted, a fin fell off and the liquid went murky. Someone said instead of watching a tiger shark hunting for dinner it was like entering Norman Bates' fruit cellar and finding Mother embalmed in her chair. Adding bleach made it worse. After cleaning up it was still disgustingly green and wrinkled.'

'I don't suppose there's any chance Saatchi threw it out?' enquired Pooley.

Amiss and the baroness guffawed in unison.

'Don't be daft, hon.' said Mary Lou. 'We're talking about the asylum that's contemporary art. The Saatchi curators skinned it and stretched the skin over a fibreglass mould. The poor thing sure didn't look good. But that didn't stop fuckwits clamouring to possess it. Sir Nicholas Serota…'

'Who?'

The baroness erupted. 'You know perfectly well who he is, Ellis. He's the bloody nincompoop who will be first into my tumbril. He runs an empire of galleries including that storehouse of junk known as Tate Modern. Tat Modern more like.'

Pooley spoke slowly. 'What…happened…to…the… wretched…shark?'

'I feel we're on a postmodern journey,' said Amiss. 'We could call it *Cherchez le cadaver.*' He saw Pooley's face. 'Sorry.'

Mary Lou patted Pooley's hand again. 'Saatchi enlisted an American international celebrity dealer called Larry Gagosian, hon, and he rang around the usual suspects. Allegedly Serota offered two million bucks...'

'Of tax-payers' money,' snorted the baroness.

'...but it wasn't enough.'

'There are celebrity dealers?' asked Pooley.

'There are celebrity hairdressers,' said Amiss. 'Celebrity cake-makers. For all I know there are celebrity undertakers. Of course there are celebrity dealers.'

'The Gagosian dude isn't known as "Go-Go" for no reason,' continued Mary Lou. 'He flogged what remained of the shark to the American billionaire art collector...'

'...celebrity art collector,' put in Amiss.

'...Steve Cohen for somewhere around eight million bucks.'

Pooley looked stunned. 'There's more,' said Mary Lou. 'Hirst seems to have suffered from scruples, so he obligingly spent a few thou on a job-lot of sharks and replaced Cohen's later that year, had another stuffed, gave it some fancy conceptual bullshit name and sold it to a Korean museum for four million.'

'Scruples my fanny,' said the baroness. 'He made Cohen pay the costs of the replacement.'

'I didn't know that.'

'The only surprise is that he didn't charge the shark.' She gazed at Pooley's shocked expression with grim satisfaction. 'Oh, and incidentally, Charles Saatchi, asked some years later if refurbishing Hirst's shark robbed it of its meaning as art, replied "Completely." Needless to say he said that when he no longer owned it.' She gesticulated at the crystal jug. 'Pour some more martinis, Robert. Ellis needs sustenance to bolster his strength so as to cope with the calf.'

'Oh, yep,' said Mary Lou. 'The calf. You'd better do this, Jack. You're more up to speed on this than me.'

The baroness waited until Amiss had refilled her glass. 'Right. Now pay attention, Ellis. Our hero split a cow and a calf from nose to tail…' She paused. 'Silly me. Of course he didn't. Hirst doesn't do anything much himself other than marketing. He has an atelier, where his assistants do the actual work. Apparently at one time he had as many as a hundred.' She snorted. 'I try to maintain my sense of humour about all this, but when I hear some halfwit explaining that Hirst is merely following in the footsteps of Rembrandt, who had a stable of students and helpers, sometimes I want to explode. Rembrandt was a genius, he taught the gifted young how to emulate him and he would let them paint less important bits of some of his pictures and occasionally their copies of his work got passed off as his. But to mention him in the same breath as bloody Hirst is blasphemy.'

'True, Jack, but calm down,' said Mary Lou. 'Get on with the story.'

'He had a dead cow and calf split, exhibited each of the four halves in a separate chic vitrine and called the result *Mother and Child, Divided.* It won the Turner Prize, which, as you will know, is named after an innovative painter of genius and is awarded annually to whatever bluffer has caught the eye of the knaves and fools who dominate the contemporary art world.' She took an invigorating swallow. 'Particularly the eye of the said Sir Nicholas Serota—or Sclerota, as I prefer to call him—who's been the prize's guiding genius.

'So anyway, my cunning plan was to string up Hirst, split his cadaver and call the result *Hanged for a Calf?* Note the question mark after 'calf.' Arguing about the significance of that could keep imbecilic critics happy for years.' She shook her head. 'But then I thought leaving his corpse unadorned would represent a lost opportunity. As you know, I am a thorough woman. This would be a perfect opportunity to display a wide range of his …' As she always did when preparing to favour her listeners with her Churchillian French, the baroness paused, set her lips in an exaggerated moue and enunciated painstakingly, '…*oeuvres id-i-o-tique de plagiaire.*'

'So he's a plagiarist as well as talentless?' asked Pooley.

'Let's say his detractors point out that there's nothing he's done that someone else didn't do first. A bloke called Ernie Saunders had a preserved shark—which he'd actually caught himself—on the wall of his shop in Shoreditch in 1989, two years before young Damien even placed the order for his dead fish. It was exhibited in 2003 in a gallery run by the Stuckists under the title *A Dead Shark Isn't Art.*'

'Stuckists?'

'The Stuckists have a quaint old-fashioned view that artists should be able to draw and paint, and rightly dismiss conceptual art as pretentious, specious, nihilistic rubbish. The name is courtesy of Tracey Emin herself, who once shrieked "'tuck! Stuck! Stuck!" at an artistic boyfriend whose painting was insufficiently avant garde for her taste.'

'Did anyone buy Saunders' shark?'

'Of course not. He offered it for a bargain million quid, pointing out that would save the buyer of his pickled shark more than five mill compared to what he described as "the Damien Hirst copy", but there were no takers.'

'Hirst was a brand by then, hon,' explained Mary Lou. 'As far as the art establishment was concerned, he had a monopoly on dead fish and animals.'

The baroness emitted another snort. 'Even though a bloke called John LeKay, whom he was very close to for a while, had exhibited animal carcasses years before Hirst produced his cattle. And lent him a science catalogue showing a cow bisected lengthways which inspired *Mother and Child, Divided.*'

She leaned forward and shook her finger at Pooley. 'Then there was the sculpture, *Hymn*, a hugely enlarged version of a torso from his son's anatomy set, which bore a startling resemblance to *Yin and Yang*, an anatomical torso exhibited a few years earlier by LeKay. Hirst had a bit of a setback here. Out of the million he got for *Hymn*, he had to cough up quite a bit because the toy manufacturer and the toy designer had complained about breach of copyright.

'Now, Ellis, are you still paying attention?'

'Yes, ma'am.'

'You must remember Hirst flogging a skull covered with diamonds.'

'Now you mention it, I do. Nasty-looking, vulgar thing.'

'During the time he was most friendly with Hirst, poor old John LeKay had constructed skulls made of soap and wax and adorned them with artificial diamonds and Swarovski crystals. He sold them for around a thousand quid. Hirst had a skull made out of platinum, had someone stick about fifteen million quid's worth of diamonds on it, called it *For the Love of God* and demanded fifty mill. Didn't quite get all of that. It ended up with a consortium that included him. But don't worry about Damien. The lad's a multi-multi-multi-millionaire. Unlike John LeKay.

'Which leads me neatly to the multi-coloured spots.'

'Which you will daub all over his body,' said Mary Lou.

'Certainly not. Which I will have daubed by an assistant. I'm not one for unnecessary physical labour, as you know.'

'I'd be surprised if Hirst was the first artist to paint spots,' said Pooley.

'You mean to have spots painted in his name,' added Amiss.

'And you'd both be right. Yes, it's an old idea and yes, he wasn't any good at it. Indeed he described the few spots he painted himself as "shite." But his industrious assistants produced many hundreds of spot canvases, which have earned their employer millions.'

'At least he's honest,' said Amiss.

'Candid would be a better word, Robert. But I will admit Damien can sometimes be almost endearing. He once explained that the best spot painting "you could have by me" would be one painted by his assistant Rachel. And when an interviewer pointed out to him that other artists claimed he had stolen their ideas, Hirst's response was: "Fuck 'em all!" Why *should* he care? There's no copyright on ideas.'

'Has the art establishment ever shown any signs of worry about all this?' asked Amiss.

'Worry?' said the baroness in her best Lady Bracknell voice. 'Worry? This month that ghastly Gasgosian creature stuffed the eleven galleries he's got dotted around smart bits of the world with a global exhibition called *The Complete Spot Paintings of Damien Hirst, 1986-2011*. All the small, medium, and big spots your little heart could desire.' She emitted a heavy sigh.

'While you're at it, don't forget about Tate Britain,' said Mary Lou.

The baroness took an enormous silk handkerchief from the recesses of her kaftan, mopped her brow theatrically, breathed deeply a few times and had a draught of martini. 'I will be calm. Yes, Tate Britain! ' She breathed deeply again. 'You and I might think that since this lucky museum owns a magnificent collection of British art since 1500, it might show us the best of it. But Sclerota's in charge of that too. Last time I was there, pre-twentieth century art was restricted to a few rooms. Modern tat was rampant.' There was another heavy sigh. 'I suppose we should be grateful that Sclerota didn't insist that in this year of the Olympics, as the world focuses on London, Tat Britain should be cluttered up for five months with an enormous Damien Hirst retrospective. No. Reason has prevailed. It's Tat Modern that's hosting his rubbish. Mind you, it's having to have its floor reinforced at great expense because huge vitrines of formaldehyde and assorted animal carcasses weigh a lot.'

'You're looking baffled, Robert,' said Mary Lou.

'I just don't understand why people are taken in.'

'Having hailed the talentless as talents in the first place, their reputations are at stake. How can all these critics and curators who've hailed Hirst as a genius fess up?'

'Besides, if dealers and collectors were to admit the emperors were naked,' said the baroness, 'they'd lose their own shirts'. She sniggered. 'Did you hear that story about the arch-luvvie, the play director Sir Trevor Nunn? Apparently, he bought one of Hirst's spin paintings...'

'What are they?' asked Pooley, wearily. 'And whom did he nick the idea from?'

'You dribble paint onto a revolving surface and see what happens. Artists—including, inevitably, John LeKay—have been doing this for decades. Hirst added motors to speed up his assistants' production line. Eventually Nunn met Hirst at a party and told him he had one of his spin paintings. Hirst asked the title and the price. Now Nunn had bought this before Hirst's prices went stratospheric, so he'd paid a mere twenty-seven thousand quid. A delighted Hirst then confided that this painting was the work of his two-year-old son, with some help from a ten-year-old pal. Nunn got over his disappointment when he later sold the thing for nearly fifty thou.'

'They're all mad,' said Pooley.

'It's a madness that's made a lot of them rich. Take the case of the journalist, A. A. Gill. In 2007, he asked Christie's to auction a painting of Joseph Stalin for which he'd originally paid two hundred. When they refused, on the grounds that they didn't deal in Hitler or Stalin, the cunning sod asked if they'd sell Stalin by Hirst or Warhol and they said they certainly would. Sadly, Warhol was dead, so Gill had to make do with his mate Hirst, who agreed to paint a red nose on Stalin and signed it. It went for a hundred-and-forty-thousand.'

'I'm speechless,' said Pooley.

'Just as well,' said the baroness. 'Less competition for me.'

'We've wandered a long way from your method of disposing of Hirst, Jack,' said Amiss. 'Will he have diamonds stuck to his head?'

'Certainly not. Unlike Hirst, I'm not made of money. But I'll have his orifices stuffed with cigarette butts.'

'Why cigarette butts?' asked Pooley.

'He's flogged cabinets full of them.'

'I thought he flogged cabinets full of pills,' said Amiss.

The baroness clicked her tongue. 'He did indeed. As—again—had been done before him. Hirst and many of his contemporaries claim to be original in their use of commonplace objects, when they're just providing variations on what Marcel

Duchamp thought of nearly a century ago. They burble these days about being in the vanguard of transgressive art…'

'What's that?' asked Pooley.

'Art that pushes the boundaries and has the knickers of the bourgeoisie in a right old twist. I've nothing against that myself. I sometimes fancy a bit of transgression. However, the point is that all this was done by the Dadaists after the first war and Marcel Duchamp, whom one might term the Dada of them all, had most of the ideas that the YBAs pass off as their own. Take the Hirst Stalin. One of Duchamp's japes was to paint a moustache and goatee on a reproduction of the Mona Lisa and exhibit it. It was Duchamp who announced that objects he called "readymades" were art.' She paused. 'Well, him being a frog, he called them "*ob-jets trou-vés.*" He kicked off with a bicycle wheel and a bottle rack. Then came the urinal.

'Stop looking so depressed, Ellis. It gets worse. Duchamp bought a urinal from an ironworks called Mott, called it Fountain, signed it R. Mutt and tried to exhibit it. It was rejected, but later became the icon of conceptual art, since Duchamp's message was that anything he said was art, was art. "I declare myself an artist, and so anything I say is art is art" became an immutable law. Actually, Duchamp was making a case for artistic freedom and he was also making a joke, but the law of unintended consequences gives us Hirst and his chums and an art establishment bowing down before them.'

'Like the Israelites worshipping the Golden Calf,' suggested Pooley.

'Funny you should mention that. Hirst gold-plated a calf's hooves and horns, called it the Golden Calf, and flogged it for nine mill.'

Pooley groaned.

'Fill us in on the cigarette butts,' requested Amiss.

'Hirst branched out into butts. Standing butts and lying-down butts carefully arranged by his loyal workforce. Some of the cabinets were edged in gold to appeal to Arabs. They went for hundreds of thousands of smackers.'

Amiss sighed. 'The older I get, the more it's borne upon me that there's one born every minute.'

'In the case of Mr. Hirst,' guffawed the baroness, 'he also believes that you should never give a sucker an even break. Especially if the sucker is rich. In that regard he does have a touch of genius. He's an alchemist: he takes base metal and turns it into gold.'

'Well at least what you've been planning is pretty original, Jack. I don't think even Hirst has come up with snuff installations before now,' said Amiss.

Mary Lou laughed. 'Jack, didn't you once suggest suffocating Jeff Koons in a giant plastic inflatable penis and sticking him outside some museum?'

'I most certainly did. I settled on Washington's Museum of Crime and Punishment as the location.' The baroness looked pensive. 'But I could never decide on quite the right title for the work. Obviously, I thought of *Dick*, but I'd reserved *Dickhead* for my creation combining real bits of that Quinn bloke who won fame with the sculpture of his head made from his frozen blood.' She glanced at Pooley. 'Come on, Ellis. You're off-duty. Stop looking down your nose like a Reverend Mother who's discovered the novices having an orgy in the cloister, and choose a so-called artist to rub out.'

'It would have to be the ghastly Emin.'

'Predictable, but nonetheless a good choice. We would be well rid of her maudlin narcissistic ramblings about her gynaecological workings. How would you dispose of her?'

'Wrap her up in her unmade bed and roll it down a cliff?'

'That's a bit unimaginative by your standards, Ellis,' said Amiss. 'What's the point of reading all those crime novels if you end up with such a pedestrian method of murder. Think Edgar Wallace.'

Pooley took a small sip of his martini and concentrated hard. 'OK. Poison her pudding with the cholera bacterium and claim she caught it because of her insanitary habits.'

'But what would you call this work of art?' asked Amiss.

The brooding silence that followed was broken by the baroness. 'I have it. Crown her with a neon light flashing *Just Deserts*. And not with a double "s"'.

'I'm getting into the spirit of this,' said Amiss. 'Can we create a giant Campbell's can full of soup and drown Andy Warhol in it? And yes, yes, I know he's dead but we could exhume him.'

'And call it *You say tomato and I say die?*' suggested Mary-Lou.

'Tempting though it would be to settle scores with any number of dead frauds,' said the baroness, 'I'm a busy woman and there simply isn't enough time. We have to stick to the living.'

'Can we get back to why you've concluded that artists are the wrong targets?' asked Mary Lou. 'You've strayed a long way from where you started.'

'I know you interrogate people for a living these days, Mary Lou, but it would be a shame were this to prevent us from dallying a while in conversational byways.'

'At the rate we're going,' said Mary Lou, 'we'll never even get a glimpse of the highway.'

The baroness looked at her watch. 'Wait till we've eaten. Now where the hell is Rachel? Ring her, Robert, and tell her to hurry up. If she's not here in five minutes we'll go in to dinner without her. I'm damned if I'm going to put the artichoke and goat's cheese soufflé in jeopardy. It's taken three arguments with the chef to get it quite right. The fellow's congenitally unsound on the chili issue.'

As Amiss headed for the door with his phone at the ready, she shouted after him: 'Tell her it's an emergency: the martini jug is empty.'

Disaster was averted when Amiss' wife arrived in the bar just in time, accepted with equanimity that the baroness considered her tube train breaking down an inadequate excuse for missing martinis, and the soufflé and all that followed were such a success that even the baroness could find no fault. The marrowbone stew with herb dumplings had caused her so much ecstasy she had been moved to charge into the kitchen to congratulate everyone. In the interstices of criticising her guests for insufficiently attending to their food and wine, she listened with surprising attentiveness to Rachel's account of what life was like as a probationary teacher in a London comprehensive.

By ten p.m. the five friends had settled in the gallery and had resolved the inevitable arguments with the baroness about whether, what, and how much they wanted to drink ('You're a crowd of blasted puritans'). Pooley and Rachel were drinking decaffeinated coffee ('Wimps! The whole point of coffee is caffeine. I'll have a double espresso.') and nothing else ('Typical!'). Mary Lou and Amiss had mollified their hostess by each ordering an Americano, agreeing to help her do justice to the decanter of port, and showing some interest in her impassioned explanation as to why the traditional Portuguese manner of treading grapes was immeasurably superior to anything a machine could do. After a few minutes, Pooley leaned forward and said, 'Jack, I hate to interrupt, but I can't stay long. If there's anything else you want to tell us about, you should get on with it. I've an early start tomorrow and murderers to locate.'

Reluctantly, the baroness turned her attention away from the delights of the Douro River Valley. 'I was seeking to alert you to the destruction of art, of course. Pay attention.'

Amiss yawned. 'You're always banging on about the destruction of something.'

'What do you expect, when the Western world is going to hell?' She reached again for her glass. 'Do I not spend my life selflessly battling with the forces of anarchy?'

'You're usually leading the forces of anarchy.'

'Only on battlegrounds of my choosing,' she said stiffly. 'When it's a necessary means of getting my way. And anyway, I never defend intellectual or moral anarchy.'

'I've heard you defend blackmail and intimidation,' remarked Rachel.

'If they're my ends, they justify my means.'

Pooley was getting irritated. 'Can we cut the philosophical niceties, Jack. I'm a simple policeman. Get to it. What's up?'

'We have fought the culture wars together, my friends,' she said, waving her glass of port for emphasis. 'But we cannot rest. The forces of darkness still reign. They must be overthrown. This time it's the Satanic army of the art world that must be destroyed.'

Mary Lou looked apprehensive. 'Haven't you won enough cultural battles to justify hanging up your sword, Jack?'

'Absolutely,' said Amiss heartily. 'When you come to think of it, you've been pretty comprehensive and successful.'

The baroness threw him a contemptuous look. 'You're mistaken if you think such blatant flattery will get you off the hook, Robert. I don't indulge in false modesty…'

'You can say that again,' said Mary Lou.

'Darling, please don't interrupt her,' said Pooley. 'It only slows everything up.'

'…so I recognise that I have had some small success in routing the evil forces of political correctness at St. Martha's[2] and Paddington University.[3] And, of course, there was the Knapper-Warburton.[4] But I cannot rest upon my laurels. There's much more to be done.'

She leaned forward confidingly. 'Now, I recognise that I cannot fight and win global cultural wars. Mine have to be small canvases. Like Jane Austen's. I am not Tolstoy.'

'You're a bit more like him than Jane Austen, if I may say so,' said Amiss. 'At least in your appetites.'

She ignored him. 'So the small canvas this time is related to art. And once more I need help.'

'What kind of help?' asked Rachel.

'Stop looking so apprehensive. I'm not going to kidnap Robert. Now pay attention and I'll tell you what we have to do.'

---

2   *Matricide at St. Martha's*

3   *Murdering Americans*

4   *Carnage on the Committee*

Chapter Two

February 2012

His phone rang mid-morning. Since the caller sounded like a frantic skylark, Robert Amiss realised it had to be Petunia Stamp, the college secretary of St. Martha's. Trying without much success to make sense of the cacophony of twitters, he gathered that she was upset. He pictured the fluttering little creature—pink alice band slightly askew and chest heaving underneath some frightful knitwear appliquéd with kittens or butterflies—and wondered yet again how Baroness Troutbeck—who suffered fools appallingly—could stand her. And vice-versa.

'Take it slowly, Miss Stamp. Is something the matter?'

'It's the mistress, Mr. Amiss. The mistress. Where, oh where, is the mistress?'

Patient questioning elicited the information that the baroness had been expected back in Cambridge the previous night but had not turned up. Since she often arrived early in the morning, no one had worried until she failed to surface at the monthly council meeting. 'A council meeting, Mr. Amiss! She missed a council meeting! You know she would never miss a council meeting. And no message. No message. And she's not answering her phone. Something terrible must have happened to her. What will we do? Should I send for the police?'

'Leave it with me for the moment, Miss Stamp. If anything's happened to her, it would probably be here rather than in

Cambridge. I'll investigate and get back to you. And don't worry. You know she's the toughest of tough old birds.'

Interpreting Miss Stamp's silence as an indication that she didn't know whether to be comforted by this undoubted truth or horrified by his *lèse-majesté*, he said goodbye in what he hoped was a manly reassuring voice and rang off.

'Sorry to have got your PA to rout you out of a meeting, Mary Lou, but it's urgent.'

'I was interviewing a grumpy poet for tonight's programme and was glad to have an excuse to get rid of the asshole. What's up? You sound agitated.'

'It's contagious. Miss Stamp's been on the phone in a right old state because she can't find Jack. And I admit to being worried. She didn't turn up for this morning's council meeting. And they can't get hold of her.'

'Hell, I'm worried! That never happened during my time at St. Martha's. Never ever.'

Amiss got up and began to pace. 'That's what's troubling me. Jack's reliability and punctuality are positively aggressive.'

'Are you thinking what I'm thinking?'

'Car crash?'

'Precisely. The way she drives it's a miracle she's never had one.'

'But if she was in hospital she'd have had ID and St. Martha's would know by now.'

'Unless Myles was down as next-of-kin. And they wouldn't have been able to find him. Isn't he still in Iraq?'

'Last time I heard. But she wouldn't have named Myles. He's away too much.'

'Supposing…?'

'Really bad crash and a fire?'

'Yep.'

'Oh, God, Mary Lou. Of course it's possible. What'll we do?'

'I'll get Ellis to put someone on to it. It shouldn't take long. It would have to have been an accident on the North Circular or the M11.'

'Unless she went by a scenic route?'

'With a motorway available on which to do a ton?'

'Sorry. Dumb idea.'

'But then of course there's the other horrible possibilities.'

'Heart attack? Stroke? Burglars?'

'That sort of thing. I'll ask Ellis to send someone round to her flat and will be back to you as soon as I hear anything that counts as news.'

◇◇◇

'You're supposed to be a crime writer,' Amiss said to himself crossly. 'Think of a benign reason why she's disappeared.' He thought of the baroness' propensity for pursuing even unlikely potential conquests—male and female—as well as of her greed for all the good things of life, but then he thought of her sense of duty and her fierce loyalty to St. Martha's. He made a vain attempt to get back to work, but finding himself looking as blankly at the screen as it looked at him, he decided to engage in displacement activity. With Radio 4 talking at him of all manner of political and cultural controversies that he could hardly take in, he attacked the kitchen belligerently and tidied up everything in the flat he could find to tidy. Resisting the temptation to bother Ellis Pooley, he forced himself to sit down at the computer, pay bills, and answer emails. He rang Miss Stamp again, found her frantic, failed to steady her, went out for a walk, phone in hand, made an unnecessary visit to the supermarket to buy unnecessary food and went home and tried to interest himself in Sky News. But Middle Eastern tensions, domestic rows about public expenditure cuts, and a hurricane threatening American cities failed to do the trick. 'I've been so worried,' he told his wife when she got home, 'that I thought of taking my mind off Jack by giving Plutarch a bath.'

Rachel looked at the fat feline sprawled across the rug. 'That would have been a suicide mission.'

'I know. I know. That's why I never bathe her. But it would certainly have distracted me.'

'Phone Ellis.'

'I don't want to seem to be fussing. He'll be doing what he can. Mary Lou would have called if there was news.'

'Oh, for heaven's sake, Robert. Impossible person though Jack is, we're all very fond of her and you and Ellis have been through so many wars together that you're blood brothers. Phone him. Now!'

'He's virtually certain that she can't have had a crash on the way to Cambridge,' Amiss reported. 'There were only half-a-dozen during the relevant period and everyone involved has been identified.'

'Has he had her flat checked?'

'Yes. A neighbour had a key. Nothing suspicious. And her car's gone. He was flummoxed and wondering whether to get her reported as a missing person.'

'She wouldn't like that if she'd simply gone AWOL.'

'But she wouldn't have gone AWOL when she was due at that meeting. It wasn't as if it was even just routine. She'd mentioned to me there was a row brewing about something or other which she had to resolve. She was trying to decide whether the appropriate tactic was conciliation or repression. You know Jack. She was looking forward to it.'

'So he'd better have her reported as a missing person, then.'

'That's what I told him. No choice.'

'How are you?'

'Miserable. Scared. Edgy.' He gave a bleak laugh. 'Like Tracey Emin. Come on, wife. Take me out for a walk and a drink and try to get my mind onto something other than that the most likely explanation is that Jack Troutbeck's dead.'

It was after eight o'clock the next morning. Amiss had given Rachel breakfast and had walked her to the tube, assuring her unconvincingly that he would call on his innate male ability to compartmentalise, avoid tormenting himself about Jack, and get some work done. Having instructed himself to hold off until nine from ringing Pooley, he looked at newspapers on-line and found himself reading the same paragraphs over and over again and checking his watch every few minutes. At half past eight, when the phone rang, he jumped up so energetically that he knocked over his coffee and the dregs spread over his keyboard. He paid no attention but grabbed the receiver. Plutarch, ever alert to the main chance, seized the opportunity to leap on his chair and curl herself into a contented marmalade circle.

'It's Ellis. No news, I'm afraid.'

'I'm sort of relieved.'

'I know what you mean.'

'What are the theories?'

'We haven't got any. We're still searching for the car. And no one here's much interested. I've got someone going through all the routine procedures with the help of her secretary: photographs, credit card details, habits, places she frequents and so on. We got hair from her London bathroom so we'll have her DNA soon. But there's no sense of urgency about this. My colleagues think academics and peers are all dotty anyway, so she's just some old bird who's wandered off somewhere on a whim. Maybe with amnesia.'

'I thought of that. But it wouldn't explain why she didn't answer her phone.'

'It's a very long shot when you know her. But if you don't… Anyway, Jim'll be back from his Interpol meeting tomorrow and he'll take it seriously. Until then there isn't much I can do.'

'OK,' said Amiss, trying to conceal the fear in his voice.

'*Courage, mon vieux*,' said Pooley. 'Think of what she's come alive out of in the past. Nine lives and all that.'

'She's used most of those up,' said Amiss gloomily.

The phone rang an hour later. Having dried his keyboard and tried vainly to make it work, Amiss had been out to the computer shop and was back in business.

'Don't let me interrupt if you're writing.'

'Oh, for heaven's sake, Mary Lou.' As he stood up and began pacing, Plutarch again took possession of his chair. 'Surely you've learned by now that most writers are desperate for distraction. By this time most mornings, I've managed to postpone starting a new chapter by answering emails that could have waited for hours and reading several newspapers on the net on the spurious grounds that I need to stay in touch with reality. If you hadn't called I might have been driven to iron a shirt.'

She didn't respond.

'And, of course, I'm worried sick about Jack.'

'That's why I rang. So am I. And I keep thinking about that dinner at ffeatherstonehaugh's. She was so right. I feel a bit ashamed. I agreed with her but I haven't done anything since to challenge the pernicious orthodoxy she's complaining about and, of all of us, I'm the gal who should.'

'But then you want to keep your job, don't you?'

'Yeah. Same old excuse everyone uses. You toe the line or you're identified as a heretic. And we all know nothing good happens to heretics. Ellis had a bit of a go at me on the way home that night for not standing up to the thought police and speaking my mind. You know when he gets priggish?'

'Don't I just!'

'He went on about the courage of one's convictions and that sort of thing. So I asked him when he last bit his tongue when a superior officer told him to do something he thought stupid or wrong—as opposed to actually immoral, which Ellis would die rather than countenance.'

'Don't tell me. That same day?'

'The day before, it turned out. Honesty is one of my guy's many saving graces.'

Amiss paced on. 'There isn't much we can do anyway, is there? Jack was calling us to arms, but the enemy is widely dispersed and we seem to lack either weapons or troops.'

'I guess we could do a bit of chipping away here or there when we get a chance. I can try to get more of a voice in arts programmes for the good guys. And if you decide to do a novel about that world, maybe you can make a difference.'

'Hah! Do you know how many copies the first one sold? Or what my advance was on this one? And before you ask, I'd have to be a few drinks in before I'd be able to bring myself to tell you. If I didn't do some journalism we'd be in complete penury. I'm relying on Rachel to hurry up and become one of those super-teachers who're brought in to turn around sink schools and are rewarded with six-figure salaries and titles.'

'Don't they have to work hundreds of hours a week?'

'She'll cope.'

'Might you seriously have a go at the art world?'

'If Jack comes back. This morning, not being able to write, I've been reading up on some of what she was going on about. Here's something from an open letter the Stuckists wrote to the benighted Serota some years back. It was a sensible, civil criticism of postmodernism.'

'Oh, holy shit,' groaned Mary Lou. 'Post-bloody-modernism rears its horrible head again. That's the incomprehensible fashionable gibberish that drove me out of academia. I hate meeting it in my new line of work. What's it supposed to mean in this context?'

'Search me. It seems to embrace all the skill-free stuff that can be done by people who couldn't paint a house or sculpt a ball out of plasticine. You know, the stuff Jack was moaning about. Along with pointless performance art, people being videoed picking their noses and all that kind of thing.'

'Postmodern almost always means waste of space and trashing of the admirable.'

'The Stuckists' view. They suggested to Serota that postmodernism…hang on a second, I was just reading it.' He leaned across Plutarch, who snarled and extended a claw. 'That postmodernism was "a cool, slick marketing machine where the cleverness and cynicism of an art which is about nothing but itself, eviscerates emotion, content and belief." The Brit artist, they went on, seemed uninterested in vision or insight, merely in maintaining "his or her media kudos in the art brat pack.'"

Amiss resumed pacing. 'They sent this to Serota for comment along with a manifesto called *Remodernism*, which called for a new spirituality in art, culture, and society to replace postmodernism's spiritual bankruptcy. Mind you, it admittedly was full of heresies like the proposition that art that has to be in a gallery to be art isn't art.'

'And Serota's response?'

'That they wouldn't be surprised to learn that he had no comment on the letter or the manifesto.'

'What a contemptuous shit! Well, that really puts him on my hate list.'

'Mine too. Then they had an exhibition of paintings in Liverpool that—from what I've seen on the net—included plenty of interesting and talented stuff. They offered the Tate a hundred-and-sixty paintings allegedly worth £500,000. The donation was turned down...hang on...I have to navigate around Plutarch to find the primary source.'

Cautiously, he once more leaned across the cat, who took noisy umbrage. 'Bloody animal. You'd think the mouse I was clicking on was a real one being wrenched from her slavering mouth. I've only just evaded serious injury.

'Anyway, the offer was rejected by Serota, who told them portentously that Tate curators and trustees felt the work lacked sufficient quality "in terms of accomplishment, innovation or originality of thought to warrant preservation in perpetuity in the national collection." The bugger didn't mention any conflict of interest, like that the curators and trustees were likely to have taken a dim view that many of the exhibits satirised Serota and the bloody Tate.

'If he'd any sense of humour he'd have accepted and displayed their most famous image of him, called *Sir Nicholas Serota makes an Acquisition*. It shows him smiling maniacally behind a large pair of red knickers on a washing line, asking himself: "Is it a genuine Emin (£10,000) or a worthless fake?"'

'Were the knickers clean?'

'Yes.'

'So I guess they couldn't be authentic.'

'What a pro you are, Mary Lou. You always get to the heart of the matter. Or, on this occasion, the gusset.'

Rachel came through the door late that afternoon just as Amiss was coming off the phone. 'Any news?'

He nodded. 'Not about Jack. But there are two more mysterious disappearances that could conceivably be related if your imagination is active enough, since Jack actually was trashing their reputations over dinner last month. They're an art dealer and a museum big shot.'

'What? Who? Charles Saatchi and Sir Nicholas Serota?'

'No. Jason Pringle and Sir Henry Fortune. I seem to remember Jack said they were dreadful, corrupt old queens.' He paused and scratched his head. 'Well, if the manager of Pringle's gallery is right, they're now missing, dreadful, corrupt old queens.'

'Any details?'

'No. Ellis will be in touch when he's talked to Jim. It's just more waiting. Be a pal and take my mind off it. Distract me. How was your day? Did you do what we talked about last night?'

'It was grim. Grim, grim, grim. And only incidentally because I was worried about Jack.' He saw her expression and led her to the armchair. She squealed, 'No, Robert, I can't sit on that till I've changed. She's been moulting all over it.' Rachel glared at Plutarch, who was oblivious, for after an ill tempered period of exile, she had regained possession of Amiss' typing chair.

Amiss looked guiltily at the protective covering that Plutarch had earlier succeeded in dragging aside. 'Sorry. I didn't notice she'd done that. I'll sort it out while you change and I'll get you a drink. White wine?'

'The way today's gone, I feel more like cyanide. But not for me. For some of my colleagues.'

By the time Rachel emerged from the bedroom in t-shirt and jeans and minus make-up, Amiss had managed to remove the worst of the fur, had ejected Plutarch into the garden where she was stalking small vulnerable creatures, some particularly soothing Mozart was playing softly in the background, and the ice-bucket held a decent Sancerre. Rachel sat down and managed a wan smile as she accepted a glass.

'What was the worst of today, darling? Did another one bite you?'

'No. It was violence-free and I actually had a few classes where the majority paid some attention. It was colleagues who sapped my spirit.'

'Go on. Tell all.'

'I can't find any way of stopping that blasted feline-worshipper…'

'The RE teacher?'

'Yes. Maureen. Not that there's either much religion or much education in what the silly cow offers the kids. It's all about peace and love and inclusiveness and celebrating each other's festivals and avoiding anything that might offend anyone, which seems to mean mentioning anything to do with Christianity, which being the majority religion, is apparently inherently offensive to minorities.'

'Judaism's OK, then?'

'Don't be absurd. Judaism's always worse with people like Maureen. She's got the kids doing a project about suffering Palestinians in Gaza. It seems to involve quite a lot of work with felt hearts and pebbles. She went on about it at some length and all I can say is that she doesn't seem to have what one might call a nuanced view of what's going on in the Middle East. In fact her take on it would probably go down great down at the local mosque.'

'You didn't mention…?'

'Being Jewish? I certainly did not. I'm trying to avoid her, not start another row. She was the one I fell out with in my first week because I got cross when she told me there was nothing more important to teach children than that man-made climate change was about to destroy the planet. Do you remember? I said it wasn't proven that it was man-made, that frightening

children didn't seem to me to be a good idea, and that really I
thought we'd be better off making them literate and numerate?
I thought she'd have a stroke.

'Unfortunately, our shared experience as cat-owners brought
her back to speaking to me today. She insisted on showing me
a dozen photos of her little treasures and expressing her disappointment that I haven't yet shown her one of dear Plutarch.
Why I was ever fool enough to admit I lived with a cat I can't
imagine. In future, I intend to be a denier.'

'You couldn't just mention that Plutarch is a vile step-cat
thrust upon you through no fault of your own?'

'That would seem disloyal. After all, when I accepted you
for better or worse I knew what that entailed in the cat depart-
ment.' As if on cue, a screech came from the next-door garden.
'Get away, you horrible animal. Leave that bird alone. Oh, no!
You murdering beast!'

Amiss and Rachel looked at each other and shrugged.
'Another one bites the dust,' said Amiss wearily. 'Go on.'

'That wasn't the worst of today. It was the art that got me
depressed.'

'Art?'

'I'd been thinking about what Jack had said about that night,
so I asked my best class what they knew about art and artists.
Do you know, there wasn't one of them that had ever been
to a gallery. And I drew complete blanks with Michelangelo,
Leonardo da Vinci, Turner, and any other obvious candidates
I tried on them.'

'Did they know there were such things as artists?'

'A couple of them had seen religious pictures in church. That
was about it.'

'You mean they hadn't even heard of Damien Hirst.'

'No. But three of the girls had seen Tracey Emin on the telly
talking about her abortion and thought she was great.'

'Oh, dear.'

'So at the staff meeting after school I said I felt they weren't
being much exposed to beauty and asked if it would be possible

to take them to the National Gallery some afternoon. My God, you'd have thought I'd suggested a brothel. And a brothel three hundred miles away on an ice-floe full of expiring polar bears at that.

'First, the deputy head began to explain how many staff would have to be with me by way of back-up. He droned on about risk assessments. Of course I knew there was a lot of bureaucracy involved in the simplest school trips, but this was beyond belief. We'd have to be prepared for all kinds of weather, transport-related problems, predictable hazards, accidents, misbehaviour in the gallery, paedophile security guards, and God knows what else. We'd have to have at least three people in attendance with first-aid qualifications and there would have to be a precise breakdown of responsibilities.'

She rubbed her forehead wearily. 'Honestly, these kids are fifteen, not five. I was tempted to—but didn't—point out that they're mostly roaming the streets on a Saturday night getting drunk and laid and that broad daylight in Trafalgar Square was probably pretty safe by comparison.'

There came an ear-splitting yowl and the sound of something heavy crashing against the kitchen door. 'Tom from down the road trying to impose his authority yet again, I'd guess,' said Amiss as he got up to investigate. 'He's pretty good at hot pursuit.'

Rachel lay back and closed her eyes as Amiss went into the garden, broke up the fight, chased the tom away, and threw a furious Plutarch into the kitchen. 'When will you grasp that you shouldn't take on something half your age and twice as fit, you stupid creature?'

There was a yowl as he investigated a bloody ear. A louder one as he cleaned it with antiseptic was accompanied by an expletive from Amiss. By the time Plutarch had been calmed down, fed and watered and had accompanied Amiss back to the living room, Rachel had been rejuvenated by a refreshing nap. She looked with distaste as the cat made a beeline for the back of the sofa, leaped to the top, and hung out of it. 'I haven't asked you for ages, Robert, but I don't suppose there's any chance Plutarch's owner is likely to get out of jail soon, is there?'

'He's not even up for parole in the foreseeable future. Unless they change the law drastically, I'm afraid Plutarch is a life sentence. Of course, that's her life, not yours.'

'I always hoped that Jack would take her on.'

'It came up in conversation recently. She said she'd love to have her back at St. Martha's for a holiday, but that sadly she'd made too many enemies. Apparently peeing in the piano was such a bad breach of etiquette that even Jack was powerless in the face of public opinion.'

'You tread on my dreams,' said Rachel. He gave her a hug. 'It's OK,' she said. 'It's OK.'

'Anyway she can't have more than ten years left, darling, and she's much better than she was. It's ages since she climbed the curtains or managed to open the fridge.'

'When you say better, you mean slightly less athletic.'

'And a bit mellower. For instance, she hardly ever bites and the scratches are positively gentle.' Rachel looked at the new plaster on the back of his hand. 'Special circumstances this evening. You'd be angry if you'd had your ear chewed by a tomcat.'

'I expect I would. All right. Forget I mentioned it. It was a moment of weakness.'

'So back to your art expedition.'

'Ah, yes. The doomed art expedition. "What's the point anyway?" asked the head of English. "It'll be wasted on them. They don't care about art."

'I was opening my mouth to suggest that this might be related to no one having ever bothered to show them any, when Maureen pointed out that it would be offensive to Muslim students to show them figurative art. I pointed out that only the most conservative of Islamic clerics regarded that as sinful, and she said it would be culturally insensitive to run the risk. Another colleague asked why I should choose somewhere as passé as the National Gallery? Surely the kids deserved to see something more relevant to their lives? What could the Renaissance mean to them? And yes, she suggested Tate Modern. And she's the deputy head of history.

'I said I thought they could do with a little more sense of the past, and there was silence. It was becoming clear that the consensus was that I am a pathetic, naïve nuisance. Then the head gave me his full attention and said, "Rachel, of course it's excellent to see a newcomer with such enthusiasm. And, yes, the world would be a better place if we could move beyond the curriculum. But we must be realistic. These children will do well to scrape a few exams and get low-grade jobs. I don't think we should give them ideas beyond what is likely to be their station. My advice to you is to teach to the test. Yes, that's what the job is all about. Teach to the test. Teach to the test."'

Amiss got up, sat on the arm of her chair, and put his arm around her. 'Do you feel like quitting?'

'No, I feel like fighting. But on a ground of my own choosing. No one can make much of a difference at my level without support from the top. I need to keep my head down, pass my probation period, and find myself a job in a school run by people who encourage aspiration and achievement.'

The phone rang and Amiss rushed to it. 'Ellis. Yes…Of course there must be a connection…It's much too much of a coincidence. Idiots…OK, I'll do that...Yes, of course…Straightaway.'

'Ellis still can't persuade anyone that there could be a link,' he told Rachel. 'He reckons if I tip off the press anonymously and get them speculating, it might help. Let me just hunt out my cloak and my dagger while I think of some way of leaking that doesn't make me seem like a complete nutter.'

Chapter Three

Around the time Miss Stamp had first been twittering at Amiss, Jack Troutbeck had woken up in an unaccustomed state of befuddlement. Instead of hurling herself out of bed to attack the day, she opened her eyes slowly, but since she was in pitch darkness, that didn't help. She could remember getting into her car in London to drive to Cambridge and then an arm coming from behind her with something that smelled sweet. 'Bloody hell,' she said to herself. 'Chloroform! How quaint.'

Sitting up, she flailed around looking for a lamp or a light switch: finding neither, she threw back her head and bellowed, 'Where the hell am I? Someone put on the light.'

Someone obliged almost immediately, and neon lighting flooded the room. A few seconds later it went off again, then on again, giving the baroness no time to see anything except that she was in small, plain room. After a couple of minutes of flickering, she shouted irritably, 'Stop doing that, for Christ's sake.'

'Feerst say please,' ordered a disembodied, guttural voice.

The baroness started. 'Who and where the hell are you?' The lights continued to flicker. 'I said stop doing that,' she yelled.

'I say you feerst say please, Laidee Troutbeck.'

'So you did. Please stop doing that whoever you are.' The lights stopped flickering.

'You thanking me.'

'That's pushing it,' she snarled.

'You thanking me or light go on off again. In o-maj.'

'In what?'

'O-maj. Martin Creed.'

'Martin Bloody Creed? Turner Prize.' The baroness groaned. 'I remember. He won with *The Lights Going On and Off*, didn't he? Now would you kindly explain what has brought about this elaborate practical joke?'

'I explain later. Maybe.' As the lights began to flicker again, the baroness muttered 'Thank you,' with a bad grace, and they stayed on.

'Now why am I here and who are you?'

'You prisoner. No escape or you want crazy Albanian kill you. They look to you, they listen you all time, all day, all night. Have knives. Machine guns.'

The baroness looked around her, observed that there was a CCTV camera and that the only window appeared to be covered with corrugated iron, tested one door that led to a windowless bathroom and another which was firmly locked. She guessed she was in a portacabin.

'I see. And who is my genial host?'

'You know who I am, Laidee Troutbeck.'

'It's Oleg, isn't it?'

'I Sarkovsky.'

'Oleg, I know we parted brass rags…'

'What means this?'

'I know we had a row, but is that a sufficient reason to kidnap and imprison me? And, indeed, to address me so formally.'

'Situation formal. You discover later. Now, you wait.'

'For what?'

'It is secret.' He sniggered. 'You say much. Now I say. I deep also. And busy man. I go. Goodbye.'

The baroness' rant to her friends about the iniquities of Sir Henry Fortune and Jason Pringle had included the information that Fortune was regarded by the deferential art world as a person of such eminence that even Sir Nicholas Serota himself could not have looked down on him. True, he had never been in charge of a major art collection, but he made sure everyone knew that his record in running fashionable museums abroad was second to none. He had managed to get himself appointed to curate several major exhibitions in British museums and also served as an international artistic adviser to a variety of galleries and arts councils with the occasional visiting professorship thrown in. An invaluable committee man who could be relied upon to know who would be the winners in any internecine fighting in the art world, his complete lack of artistic integrity served him well. The baroness had actually remarked that whatever you thought of bloody Sclerota, he seemed genuinely to believe his own noxious propaganda, while Fortune would have his own granny cleft in twain and exhibited in formaldehyde if that won him another cushy job.

Sir Henry was very thick with Pringle, with whom he'd been an item since they were students at the Courtauld Institute. It was reputed that it was Pringle who first gave him the nickname 'Bubbles,' which he hated but which stuck, even now that his red curls had long departed. Although it was common gossip that Pringle's insatiable appetite for redheads and Fortune's less frequent mooning after darkish teenage hunks occasionally caused massive rows in which there was much accusation and counter-accusation about gingers and rent-boys, their partnership seemed rock solid. As unkind people said, they had too much in common ever to split, particularly their shared view of art as a means to promote Fortune and Pringle. It was no accident that Fortune frequently acquired for one or other of his museums a work by a young artist whom Pringle was promoting—a guaranteed method of putting prices through the roof. When he was in London, Fortune stayed with Pringle in his Kensington penthouse and, loyally, they talked each other up at launches and art fairs. Pringle might have lacked the Midas touch of Charles Saatchi, but he was rich. He gave disproportionate but not exclusive attention to those he fancied and had a keen and cynical eye for artistic trends.

The police had been told that although both men were to speak on Thursday night at the opening of an exhibition in Pringle's gallery of works by his latest wunderkind, neither had shown up and both were unreachable by phone. Mid-morning on Friday, leaving Serafina, the intern, in charge, Allegra, the gallery manager, had gone to Pringle's apartment and had rung the door-bell, but though she had brought with her the spare key her boss kept in the office, she was too scared of what she might actually find to put the key in the lock. When she consulted the hall porter, he told her it was more than his job was worth to leave his post. 'If you want my advice, Miss, though don't quote me, you should call the cops.'

When she got back to the gallery Allegra nervously called 999, but she was hesitant and slightly incoherent, and initially she was dismissed as a bit of posh totty who was getting worked up about nothing.

After midday, there was a near-hysterical call from the head of an art college. Where was Sir Henry Fortune? He was supposed to be giving the awards to the prize pupils and making a speech, but staff, students, parents, and notables had already been waiting half-an-hour and there had been no word. If Allegra didn't know where to find him, what was to be done?

Allegra couldn't help the lunch date stood up by Pringle either, but the two calls had stiffened her spine, and after consultation with Serafina, who was even posher than she was and much more confident, she rang 999 and made a fuss.

By late afternoon, the spare key had been picked up and by half past six Pooley had a report. There was no one in Pringle's apartment and no sign of anything untoward. Two suitcases in the spare room with Fortune's name tags had been unpacked and his clothes were neatly hung-up and put away. A half-drunk bottle of champagne in the fridge suggested they might have had a quick stiffener before leaving for the gallery, even if there were no glasses to be seen. The porter recalled them leaving and said he assumed that, as usual, they would be hailing a black cab. He also unbent sufficiently to mention that Pringle's cleaner had been upset this afternoon that he had neglected to leave her wages on the kitchen table.

The police were sufficiently impressed by the grandeur of Pringle's apartment and by his friend's knighthood to spread the story around when they got back to the Yard. Pooley had been making so much fuss about the baroness that he was one of the first officers to hear from the missing persons unit that another nob—indeed two nobs—had disappeared. However, his attempts to suggest any link had fallen on unreceptive ears.

He and Amiss were disappointed that the newspapers and news channels he had called had shown little interest. However, the evening newspaper ran with a small story by its arts correspondent speculating on why Fortune and Pringle were not to be found. Had those indefatigable patrons of the arts been deflected from the gallery because they were in hot pursuit of some startling new talent with which to engender shock and awe in the art world?

The police called the wunderkind whose big event had been marred by his mentors' absence to enquire if he'd any useful information. It took his assistant some time to fetch him, for they were immersed in the difficult process of making a video showing his struggles to make a video, and at the time of the call, the artist was standing on his head in the nude, trying to keep a banana wedged in his bum while balancing a basket of tropical fruit on his feet. He had given up on trying to hold a pineapple in his mouth, for even with some judicious surgery, the fruit had proved wholly uncooperative. When the phone rang, he had just got his teeth around a large plum. It hurt a bit because of the lacerations caused by the pineapple, but he'd got a good grip on it.

He was furious at having to take the call, but he hid his disgruntlement, bemoaned his inability to help, and instead expressed his gratitude for all that these two inspirational legends of the art world had done for him and people like him. He did not mention that he thought Pringle treated him like a whore.

Back at work, he resumed his earlier position with some difficulty, the assistant jammed the banana and plum back into position, balanced the basket on his feet, and covered the entire ensemble with imitation snow flakes. The theme was climate change but the artist was becoming desperate at his inability to think of a knock-out title. For the moment they were running with *Climate Carmen* (after Carmen Miranda). Then he had a moment of inspiration. He spat out the plum. 'Not a banana,' he cried. 'What was I thinking of? Buy a feather. Now.'

His assistant looked at him in bewilderment.

'A feather?'

'A feather.'

'What kind of feather?'

'Oh, for fuck's sake,' cried the wunderkind as he tumbled to the floor. He sat up and ran his fingers through his plentiful red curls. 'A feather from a cock. And make sure it's a big one.'

'From a cock?'

'Yes, you idiot. A cock. Like in hen. I've just realised this work is to be called *Cocktail Climate*. We'll substitute the feather for the banana.'

The assistant's weariness and irritation left him in an instant. 'Oh...My...God!' he said. 'That's perfect. You'll be a dead cert for the Turner.'

◇◇◇

The media got good and interested on Friday evening, when Jake Thorogood's editor, who had been expecting copy from him all day for his Saturday art column, eventually tracked down his current squeeze and found she hadn't been able to get hold of him since Friday morning. They had been having a leisurely breakfast when Thorogood answered the doorbell. He had stuck his head back in the kitchen and said he'd be back in a moment and never came back at all. She thought she'd heard a car driving off, but couldn't be sure. What she was sure of was that Thorogood wasn't given to leaving the house in February clad only in a nightshirt and silk dressing gown.

Thorogood worked for a major liberal newspaper, was an able intellectualiser of modish opinions, was often photographed sharing a joke with art-world celebrities, and was therefore one of the media's own. Even the tabloids were interested, for they quickly discovered that Thorogood, Fortune, and Pringle had together made the reputation of Anastasia Holliday, the leggy blonde who had recently made abject art the talk of the town with her inventive ways of using her bodily fluids and her unself-conscious Australian coarseness. Attempts by journalists to get hold of Holliday drew a blank, and it was not long before she had also been added to the missing persons file. No one had seen her since her brief attendance at the event at Pringle's gallery at which he and Fortune had been no-shows.

Grave articles in the fashionable press about all that was owed to these icons of artistic experimentation had as their counter-point pages of photographs in the tabloids of work the subs particularly despised as confidence tricks. As Amiss observed to Rachel, one mightn't think much of the popular press, but when it came to seeing that talentless rubbish was talentless rubbish, the lowliest hack was likely to show better judgement than the panjandrums of the art establishment. He recalled the baroness referring to Thorogood as the Judas Iscariot of art criticism, her contention being that he knew what was good and beautiful but didn't have the balls or integrity to stay loyal to it.

The art world, the press, and the police were now as one in believing that some lunatic had a grudge against contemporary art. Was there somewhere some more traditional artist running amok? A stern finger of suspicion was pointed at the Stuckists, a few of whom were pulled in for questioning. The disappear-ance of the baroness confused the picture and therefore she was mostly ignored. Hysteria went up a notch when Dr. Hortense Wilde's husband said she'd gone out to the garden centre first thing Saturday morning and hadn't been seen since.

'Dear God,' said Amiss, when Pooley rang him. 'I know her. Ghastly woman.'

'How do you know her?'

'Met her at the in-laws with Jack the other week. Compli-cated story.'

'We need a council of war, Robert. You seem to know a lot about these people. Jim's back from Paris. I'll find out how he's fixed and get back to you.'

'Now Hortense Wilde's gone missing,' Amiss told Rachel when she got home.

'You're kidding.' She shuddered. 'That was a really appalling evening.'

'It sure was.'

◇◇◇

The evening had started well. Apart from that brief period when her daughter's wedding had caused Dr. Simon to turn into an hysterical seeker after perfection, Amiss was very happy with Rachel's clever, warm-hearted parents. The baroness clearly liked the house, which was sprawling, comfortable, and bookish. She enthused about their garden and approved their brand of gin. She and Martin Simon turned out to have a common interest in military history, from which they moved on to great war paintings and art in general. As Amiss fetched the baroness another drink, the doorbell rang. 'Hannah will get that,' said Simon. 'It's just our new neighbours. They moved in today and we thought it would be kind to offer them dinner. They seem pleasant enough.'

Hortense Wilde was long and thin with a face so elongated that she reminded the baroness of a Modigliani. Over drinks, there were polite questions about where she and her rather crumpled husband had moved from and why. The baroness, on her best behaviour, had affected interest even though she wasn't the centre of attention. The trouble started over dinner when Hortense asked Amiss what he did. 'Er, I've had quite a few jobs,' he said, 'but most recently, I've been writing a bit.'

'What do you write?'

'I do some journalism, but mainly I'm trying to concentrate on novels. Crime novels.'

'And are you published?'

'Yes. My first came out a few months ago and I'm finishing the second.'

She laughed tinnily. 'I'm afraid I won't have read you. I don't go in for popular fiction. Is it all sex and sadism?'

'No, it isn't,' said the baroness, who had suddenly lost interest in the conversation going on to her left. 'Robert doesn't write penny dreadfuls. He writes entertainingly for intelligent people.'

'I'm sure he does,' said Wilde. 'But I'm afraid I'm more interested in serious issues.'

'Here's a serious issue then,' said the baroness, who was already spoiling for a fight and thought she might have spotted a promising foe. 'Why is the art world peddling so much crap these days? Robert and I were in Tat Modern today and it was crammed full of rubbish. Now admittedly, that's to be expected from the gormless artistic elite. But Martin told me a story just now about how far this disease has spread. Go on, Martin.'

Martin Simon, always a man to avoid any kind of confrontation, looked nervously at her. 'Oh, I don't know, Jack. Hortense mightn't be interested.'

'Any sane person should be interested. Nay outraged. Go on. Go on. If you don't, I'll have to give her a mangled version of it.'

'Very well,' he said meekly. 'Jack was expressing an interest in contemporary art earlier, Hortense, so I told her about visiting the new National Museum of Art in Cardiff when I was there on business last week. I was particularly taken by the work of a distinguished eighteenth-century painter called Richard Wilson. However part of one of his interesting landscapes was obscured by a huge pile of small cardboard boxes—six-and-a-half thousand to be exact, as this was a reaction to the local council's plan to build six-and-a-half thousand new houses. They were bird boxes, as the Welsh title meant something like "Birds of a feather flock together." What amused me was that they came in flat packs and had to be assembled by the museum staff.'

'It seems perfectly valid to me,' said Hortense Wilde.

'How can it?' asked the baroness. 'It's a waste of money. It requires no talent, no skill. It's utterly pointless. Surely you can see that?'

'I think perhaps I see more than you do, Jack. I'm an art historian.'

Amiss saw his parents-in-law exchanging a grimace of embarrassment. The baroness, on the other hand, wore an expression closely resembling that of Plutarch preparing to stalk a tasty victim. 'How interesting,' she said silkily. 'There are a lot of you about these days. Would I have read anything of yours?'

'I don't write for the general public.' She repeated the tinny laugh. 'I'm afraid the discourse in which I engage is above most people's heads.'

'I'll never understand academics who think they should be paid just to talk to each other,' snapped the baroness. 'Shouldn't your job be to make the obscure limpid and the profound accessible and generally help the ordinary person appreciate a great picture? Like Walter Pater or Kenneth Clark did?'

Wilde laughed again. 'I don't think either of those men left anything worth passing on to a modern generation.'

'They introduced many to truth and beauty.'

'Oh, really, Jack.' Wilde raised her hands. 'Truth!' she said, as two fingers on each hand made air quotes. 'Beauty!' she said, and repeated the gesture. 'These are really passé concepts. I am pleased to have played my part in ejecting this reactionary poison from the artistic consciousness. We have moved on from a belief in the socially constructed to an understanding of the inevitability of cultural relativism. But you wouldn't understand that unless you move in intellectual circles,' she added, with a kindly smile. 'The analysis of trauma and the psycho-sexual in the field of postmodern feminist theory, for instance…'

The baroness groaned loudly. 'Oh, God,' she said. 'Spare me that PC pseudy clap-trap.'

'Jack is nothing if not forthright, Hortense,' interjected Hannah Simon brightly. 'She is also the Mistress of St. Martha's in Cambridge, so she does move in intellectual circles. But I think it would be best if you two agreed to differ and we talked about something else.' She turned to Wilde's husband. 'We were having

such a fascinating conversation about Hampstead, Gervase, that
I didn't have time to discover what you do.'

'I'm an educational theorist.'

'An academic?'

'Yes.'

'Which side are you on?' asked the baroness.

'Sorry?'

'Which side are you on? Traditional or progressive?'

'Progressive, of course.'

Hortense Wilde looked at the baroness with ill-concealed
dislike. 'Gervase has been a seminal force in helping to lead
teachers away from notions of imparting knowledge rather than
facilitating children to find out for themselves in their learning
zone what interests them.'

'Oh, dear God,' said the baroness. 'So I've him to thank for so
dumbing down schooling that at St. Martha's we have to provide
remedial teaching for semi-literate undergraduates.'

'Now, now, Jack,' said Martin Simon. 'I know you have strong
opinions, but we don't want a falling-out.'

Amiss gave way to temptation. 'Really, Jack, I think you
should hold back on this one. My wife's a teacher,' he said to
the Wildes. 'Darling, why don't you tell Gervase and Hortense
what life is like in your school.'

'There were pools of blood on the carpet,' Amiss told Pooley.
'So naturally the following day Jack rang up without a care in
the world to rejoice about having had so much fun. I mentioned
that it was a bit difficult for the Simons to have their neighbours
roughed up, and that while they thought they were terrible
pills, they had reeled when she accused them of being Marxist
throwbacks who leeched off the taxpayer while destroying the
twin bedrocks of society and culture.'

'Good old Jack.'

'Indeed. She was thrilled to know she'd been so pithy. And
Rachel hadn't been much better. Anyway, that's Hortense.'

'Robert?'

'Yes, Ellis.'

'Has it occurred to you that since all these people have almost certainly been kidnapped by the same person, they are therefore presumably imprisoned together?'

'Dear God,' said Amiss. 'I know this is a terrible thing to think, let alone say, but wouldn't you love to be a fly on the wall?'

Chapter Four

The baroness had once idly pronounced in a House of Lords debate that everyone should be forced at school to learn vast tracts of poetry by heart lest someday they might find themselves in solitary confinement and need to ward off madness. She now had a chance to test her hypothesis. While she had always claimed to be as happy in her own company as she was joyous in her own skin, by that she meant happy reading, writing, or generally being busy without anyone else around. This prison, however, did not run to books, paper, radio, parrot, or any diversions whatsoever.

Although only soap had been provided, she had managed to stretch her ablutions out to about fifteen minutes, after which she had looked for food and drink and found that all that was there was water that had to be drunk from the tap. She was starving, and thought of demanding food, but then concluded that since Sarkovsky was torturing her for his own reasons, she would not give him the satisfaction of showing she minded.

Not being of a meditative or spiritual disposition, she found sitting on a narrow bed contemplating white walls completely boring, so she marched up and down reciting. She began defiantly with Kipling's *If*, and was relieved that she could remember all four verses. She shouted loudest the lines:

'If you can force your heart and nerve and sinew
To serve your turn long after they are gone,

And so hold on when there is nothing in you
Except the Will which says to them: "Hold on!"'

There was Marvell. She was delighted to find she still remembered 'To His Coy Mistress,' and made much of 'Let us roll all our strength, and all/Our sweetness, up into one ball:/And tear our pleasures with rough strife/Through the iron gates of life.' With Keats, she triumphed again with 'On Looking into Chapman's Homer,' making it right through from 'Much have I travell'd in the realms of gold' to 'He stared at the Pacific—and all his men/Look'd at each other with a wild surmise—/Silent, upon a peak in Darien' and doing a creditable imitation of stout Cortez.

She then fell into uncharacteristic melancholy during Byron's 'Youth and Age': 'There's not a joy the world can give like that it takes away,/When the glow of early thought declines in feeling's dull decay', and had to flog herself to get to its dismal end, but she then cheered herself up by remembering Byron had died at thirty-six and therefore didn't know what he was talking about. She raised her spirits further with Hilaire Belloc's 'Tarantella,' 'Do you remember an Inn,/Miranda?,' and John Betjeman's 'A Subaltern's Love-Song,' and when describing Miss Joan Hunter Dunn's exploits with a tennis racket, fell silent in happy recollection of a very satisfactory fling with a doubles partner in her sixth form. That triggered off an equally satisfying memory of what she had got up to with a mixed doubles partner in the local tennis club.

She was contemplating making a shot at 'The Rubaiyat of Omar Khayyam,' when she looked at the camera and decided on an experiment. Fetching the towel from the bathroom, she pushed her chair over to the corner, climbed onto it and covered the camera. Within a couple of seconds the lights began to flicker on and off again. She removed the towel: they stayed on. Sighing, she accepted she was under close scrutiny and climbed down. She had declaimed, 'Awake! For morning in the Bowl of Night/Has flung the stone that puts the stars to flight', when she had a better idea. Damn them, if they were spying on her, they might as well suffer too.

The baroness loved singing, and she had the lungs and the diaphragm for it, but she knew that when she broke into song in the presence of friends they would clap their hands to their ears and beg her to stop. She was a realist, so she pretended but didn't believe that the problem was that they were tone deaf rather than that she couldn't hold a tune.

She considered her repertoire and decided that what circumstances required were Puccini arias. She always refused to go to operas unless they were performed in the original, but her own linguistic skills were so lacking that she had the greatest difficulty in learning any lines in a foreign language, so all she could offer were short extracts. Her rendition of the noisiest bits of *Nessun Dorma* were followed by a goodly chunk of *Si, mi chiamano Mimi*, but it took the high spot of Madame Butterfly's misguided belief that Lieutenant Pinkerton would be back soon to provoke a reaction. The lights went on and off, the baroness went on singing, total darkness descended, but she reprised the passage over and over again until interrupted.

'I'll give you food if you stop singing,' said a voice in an accent that she recognised from her occasional encounters with Sarkovsky's bodyguards.

A deal was struck after five minutes of negotiation and with a clear understanding that the boss would not be told that she was being fed. The lights went on for long enough to allow the baroness to shut herself in the bathroom. After a few minutes, she heard a door open and close: the lights went on and she rushed out and grabbed the plate of food on the floor. She couldn't remember when she had last enjoyed anything as much as the goat's cheese and corn bread. She thought of her last angry meal with Sarkovsky and wished that she had taken heed of Kai Lung's wise words: 'Better a dish of husks to the accompaniment of a muted lute than to be satiated with stewed shark's fin and rich spiced wine of which the cost is frequently mentioned by the provider.' When she had finished, she lay down on the uncomfortable bed and hoped that her friends would be quick about tracking her down.

Wherever she was.

Some of her friends were trying to do just that. The council of war was held at the Pooley flat that evening. Mary Lou was stuck at work and Rachel had gone to see her parents. 'It's not that I wouldn't postpone if I could be of any use, Robert,' she'd said, 'but I can't see that I've anything to contribute. Whereas you Three Musketeers have form. Good luck.'

Amiss, Pooley, and Milton sat round the kitchen table, ate take-away pizza and drank red wine. The mood was gloomy. 'Now that Jim's back and all these others are missing,' said Pooley, 'Jack's disappearance is no longer being dismissed lightly.'

'It's got to be Oleg Sarkovsky who's behind this,' said Amiss.

'I agree,' said Pooley. 'But I got nowhere when I suggested it to the AC.'

'Oleg Sarkovsky?' asked Milton. 'Isn't he some dodgy Russian oligarch? What's he got to do with this? Hasn't she got enemies closer to home?'

'Well, of course she's got enemies, Jim,' said Amiss, pushing his almost untouched plate away. 'We're talking about Jack. But Sarkovsky's the only serious one who comes to mind at the moment. Although I don't like Sir Nicholas Serota and I doubt if he liked what she said about him in the culture debate in the House of Lords last week, he has a thick skin and plenty more pressing enemies than Jack Troutbeck. Besides, even Jack never suggested he was a criminal. Well, except culturally.'

'So tell me about this Sarkovsky.'

'You begin, Ellis.'

'We had dinner with Jack some weeks back, when you were away. She was rather worked up about the iniquities of the contemporary art world.'

'In other words,' said Amiss, 'she did a lot of ranting.'

'Eventually, it turned out that this new obsession had been inspired by her relationship with Sarkovsky.'

'Her relationship? What sort of relationship?' asked a startled Milton. 'I thought she and Myles were still an item.'

'Well, yes, when she isn't off having dalliances. Or him off adventuring in the Middle East. Which is where he is at the moment.'

'She described Sarkovsky as her walker,' said Pooley. He paused and considered. 'No, she said she was *his* walker, but then modified it to trophy.'

'As in trophy wives?' asked Milton.

'No and yes,' said Amiss. 'In such matters apparently he likes tall blondes half his age with big chests. He swaps a wife from time to time when she reaches what he considers her sell-by date. But being uneducated and sensitive about it, he was attracted by the idea of an intellectual trophy. Brain-candy, I guess. He met Jack at some social gathering where she was holding forth about the wonders of Western civilisation and presumably thought her the answer to an ignoramus' prayer.

'What with Jack being a baroness and the head of a Cambridge college, she enhanced his status just by being seen with him. But he also wanted her to educate him about culture.'

Milton was bewildered. 'Why would she do that? Isn't she too busy to be a tutor?'

'The bait was luxury, Jim. Extreme luxury. You know our Jack's a sybarite. She loves travelling in extreme comfort. And staying in the best suites in the most expensive hotels. She said we'd get the idea if we thought of a tutor on the Grand Tour with a rich, vulgar, and doltish spendthrift. They went to Venice on the Orient Express so she could introduce him to Byzantine art and architecture as well as to the Renaissance.'

'And by private plane to Rome so she could teach him some classical history,' contributed Pooley.

'And cruised around the Greek islands in his yacht so she could tell him about the origins of democracy and recite Byron at him.'

'I can see the appeal of all that,' said Milton. 'Do you want any more of that pizza, Robert?'

'No, no. Have it. What an appetite you've got tonight.'

'I'm busy.' Milton reached across and cleared Amiss' plate. 'I live alone. I forget to buy anything. I get hungry. Married blokes have wives to force them to eat, I seem to remember. Divorced ones don't.'

'It's not quite that simple, Jim. Ellis and I don't exactly have wives wearing pinnies and cooking up a storm. I imagine we can both see the attractions of a fully-staffed yacht as well as the next man. And according to Jack it was opulent in the extreme. She said rather apologetically that Sarkovsky was in the second eleven on Planet Oligarch, seeing as how—unlike Roman Abramovich, of whom he was madly jealous—he didn't own a football team and has only one yacht, which shamingly doesn't double as an aircraft carrier or have an escape capsule. It does, of course, have the obligatory helicopter pad—a convenience she took to. And she waxed pretty eloquent about the virtues of the butler and the chef on duty on board, as well as their equivalents in Sarkovsky's various houses.'

'Was he paying her as well?'

'No. Just picking up all the tabs. But she had hopes of extracting a tidy donation from him for St. Martha's.'

'So for heaven's sake, what was the problem? It sounds like a mutually satisfactory arrangement. Why would he want to kidnap her?'

'They were falling out rather often, particularly about conceptual art, which other billionaires were buying in truckloads and which she consistently ridiculed. She got the impression that he was furious that Abramovich's girlfriend had set up a centre for contemporary art in Moscow and that he was harbouring similar ambitions to do the same in St. Petersburg, where he was born. So to make sure he stayed on the artistic straight and narrow she missed no opportunity to beat him up any time he said a kind word about what she thought was crap. You know how tactless she can be.'

'I certainly do,' said Milton.

'And although she was firmly of the view that she was successfully pretending she enjoyed his company, she despised him
and it showed. If you think—as she does—that apart from low
cunning he has no intellect, it's hard to disguise. I heard her
on the phone once berating him for tastelessness and generally
taking the piss out of him about everything from his baldness
to his struggles with English, for which he seemed to have no
aptitude whatsoever. I don't think he's a man who would take
that well.'

'If people got violent with Jack every time she was tactless,'
observed Milton, 'she'd have been dead and buried a long time
ago.'

'Most people aren't Oleg Sarkovsky. Tell him, Ellis.'

'Jack asked me to find out how dodgy he was, but then refused
to take what I found out seriously enough.'

'He's a real villain, you mean?'

'As I said to Jack, Russian oligarchs made billions through
ruthlessly taking advantage of the chaos that followed the collapse of the Soviet Union. Depending on their point of view, you
could call them entrepreneurs or you could call them bandits.
Sarkovsky was never going to be Robin Hood. The trouble is he
turned out to be more like the Sheriff of Nottingham.'

'Didn't he usually lose out to Robin?' asked Amiss.

'I mean in the sense of robbing the poor for the good of the
rich. And showing no mercy. Sarkovsky was notoriously corrupt
as well as rough with his business competitors. Some of them
ended up dead.'

'What did Jack say to this?'

'That Russia in the early nineties resembled the Wild West,
and one can't judge it by the standards of Little-Moreton-on-
the-Marsh. So I added that the word was he's a bit of a psycho.
And won't brook criticism. A journalist who was on his trail
ended up dead.'

'Did she listen to that?'

'Up to a point. She listened, but then she asked how that
murder could be pinned on Sarkovsky considering Putin has

journalists rubbed out as often as he shoots bears. To which I said that it couldn't, but there were very good grounds for suspicion. Also, his most recent ex-wife is on the record accusing him of beating her up.'

'Jack's reaction to that?'

'She asked if the ex-wife's accusations had netted her an extra few tens of millions in the divorce settlement. And wanted more evidence about the deaths he's alleged to have ordered. She was procrastinating, if you ask me.'

Amiss shrugged. 'There was a golden pot at the end of the rainbow for St. Martha's, and that's always Jack's top priority.'

'Doesn't she mind where it comes from?' asked Milton.

'No. She long ago said fund-raising was prostitution and you didn't demand that your clients had good conduct medals. Just as long as they didn't give one the metaphorical clap.'

'So she ignored your advice?'

'Not completely,' said Amiss. 'I rang her just before she went with him to Marrakesh and she admitted being slightly perturbed. Myles had called her from Iraq to say he'd heard a few bad things about him from some old SAS-hand.'

'But that didn't make her cancel the trip.'

'No. "I think this might be make-or-break weekend," she said. "But for now I must fly. Like Chambers Dictionary, I'm Morocco bound."'

Milton sighed and reached for the last piece of pizza. 'And what happened in Morocco?'

Amiss took another mouthful of red wine. 'She called me on Saturday evening to explain that every prospect pleased and only Sarkovsky was vile. On the plus side, she was in the Churchill suite in La Mamounia, had seen some fine Islamic architecture, been massaged with all manner of fabulous unguents in the spa, had eaten outside in a balmy breeze, and when she rang she was sitting on her private terrace, smoking a superb cigar, drinking a fine brandy, and gazing at the enormous garden which Winston Churchill pronounced the loveliest place in the world.'

'And the minus side?'

'The food was disappointing and she couldn't get it into Sar-kovsy's thick head that Islamic art and architecture were worthy of admiration. Relations were already strained when he had a call that put him in a terrible mood. He'd a few by then and he fessed up. Turned out he'd an art adviser he'd been keeping secret from Jack because, as he put it, he didn't think she was very fresh about art and he'd secretly spent a few hundred million behind her back on Hirsts and Emins and Koons and the rest of the usual suspects. Still, she'd been troubling him with her negative comments about conceptual art so he'd had an independent evaluation of the art he'd bought through the said adviser. He'd just been told his collection had gone down drastically in value.'

'She didn't sympathise, I suppose?'

'She sure didn't. She told him it served him right. That had he bought art of intrinsic value of the kind she had been trying to educate him to appreciate, he would have a collection of which he could be proud, but that by going for the trophy shock-and-awe art recommended by people without taste or scruple, he had landed himself with a load of dross which would probably be worth nothing in ten years time. And serve him right. If he had any sense, she said, he should sell the lot now.'

'That didn't go down well?'

'It didn't. He threw a tantrum and stormed off. She retired to her magnificent suite to commune with the ghost of Churchill.'

'And what did Churchill recommend?'

'More brandy. But she was sufficiently rattled to ask me to locate Ellis and find out if he'd learned anything more about Sarkovsky. She had a feeling that he might be having business problems.' He gestured at Pooley. 'Over to you, Ellis.'

'He was indeed having business problems. I met her a couple of days after she got back to tell her to drop Sarkovsky, but she said he didn't appear at all on Sunday and had sulked all the way back to London on Monday, so that in effect they'd dropped each other. She then admitted she might be tempted if he relented and repeated an earlier offer to take her on an adventure tour up the Amazon, so I gave the unexpurgated story. There were good reasons to think he'd had a business partner blown up just because he wanted one hundred percent of the company.'

'He wasn't just getting his retaliation in first in the manner of Russian crooks?' asked Milton.

'My sources didn't think so. They're not very judgemental in Russia, but apparently they were a bit shocked because he and the business partner had been friends from childhood.'

'So how did he get away with it?'

'Bribery.'

'And the journalist who allegedly was murdered?'

'Was a young investigative reporter from the local paper who was concerned about medical supplies bound for local hospitals being hijacked on an industrial scale and diverted into the black market.'

'The link with Sarkovsky?'

'Apparently she had evidence his trucking company was involved. But once again, the police dropped the case before any charges could be brought.'

'And the wife?'

'Turns out she was backed up by the first ex-wife, who said he used to get violent when he didn't get his own way and once nearly strangled her. But, mysteriously, they both withdrew their evidence after their dogs were shot. That was the evidence that worked with Jack. "He had his ex-wives' dogs shot!" she cried. "That's it. No one who would have dogs shot deserves the benefit of the doubt. Why, he might strangle Horace if he said something rude to him. I don't mind taking risks for the sake of St. Martha's, but I'm damned if I'm going to have my parrot put in jeopardy."'

Milton laughed. 'How very Jack. But I still don't really get it, Robert. Surely if Sarkovsky was crazy and wanted to get rid of her he'd have done what Russians do and ordered a drive-by shooting or poisoning with ricin or something. He's hardly got her locked in a cellar while he decides what to do with her. I also don't get it about the others. Where do they come into it?'

Why would he have it in for them as well? Aren't they the art establishment Jack despises?'

'I don't understand either. Except that he's a psycho.'

'OK,' said Milton. 'I'll start enquiries.'

'Enquiries? Shouldn't you be breaking down the doors of Sarkovsky's houses with battering rams and giving him the third degree?'

'This is London, Robert. Not Moscow. We wouldn't get search warrants on the basis that he and Jack had a row in Marrakesh several weeks ago and that he's got a dodgy reputation. Anyway, we're not keen in the Met to make enemies of incredibly rich people who can afford top-of-the-range lawyers. But I'll talk to the AC ASAP.'

'Do you think you'll get anywhere with him, Jim?' asked Pooley.

'Very likely not. But the commissioner's away so I've no choice.'

'You'd better hurry up before Sarkovsky nabs the next one,' said Amiss.

'You don't think he's finished?'

'He's a thorough sort of bloke from all I've heard. If I were you, I'd be warning all the curators and dealers and artists and wankers in London to batten down the hatches and hide under their beds.'

Milton's phone rang. 'Yes…shit!…yes…yes…yes…why do you think it's connected?…yes…yes…yes…Try to find out if there's a connection with Oleg Sarkovsky….Oleg Sarkovsky. A London-based Russian billionaire…OK.'

He disconnected. 'We need to go back to the Yard, Ellis. An American art consultant and one of his clients has gone missing from his London hotel for a few days. Even the AC's taking it seriously now.'

Chapter Five

'What the hell's an art consultant?' asked Milton, as they sped back to the Yard.

'Give me a minute.' Pooley specd-dialled Mary Lou. 'What the hell's an art consultant, darling? Some American bloke called Chester Herblock's gone missing and that's his job title...yes... yes...yes...yes...OK...Thanks...No, no, but I think Sarkovsky's behind it...I don't know...Could be a very late night... Me too...'Bye.'

'Mary Lou says art consultants are top-of-the-range advisers hired by the rich and ignorant to make them appear discriminating. They choose the art; you pay the bill; they get a big commission. The more you pay, the bigger the commission. She's heard of Herblock. He's a mega-rich celebrity art consultant. It's a grand name for an art adviser.'

'So he could be the person who advised Sarkovsky to buy the stuff Jack loathed,' said Milton. 'OK, Ellis. Take charge. I have to go and report to the AC. Hell, I wish the commissioner wasn't away. The AC will inevitably find our theory about Sarkovsky fanciful.'

Pooley had just finished reading the reports of the disappearance of Herblock and the woman with whom he'd been staying at the Dorchester when he was told that no one could find Gavin Truss, the head of the Central London School of Art, who hadn't been seen anywhere since leaving his office for the preview party at Pringle's gallery. Pooley knew who he was. He'd seen the baroness demolish him on *Newsnight*.

The confrontation had arisen because of the baroness' allegation in her Lords speech that—because of the cancer of conceptual-ism—art schools had long since ceased teaching their students anything worth a damn and should be denied as much as a penny of taxpayers' money. Gavin Truss—who had spent a quarter-of-a-century teaching the subject and for a decade had been head of the Central London School of Art—was small and superior, with a manner and tone that—rather like the baroness— denoted his utter certainty in the rectitude of his opinions. Having had a few of her more trenchant remarks quoted at him, he sat back in his chair, tugged his little curly beard like a lucky charm, and told the presenter that Lady Troutbeck was a classic philistine in an outdated institution who pontificated about what she didn't understand. What students learned in his establishment was priceless.

'Over to you, Lady Troutbeck.'

'What do you teach them?'

'What do you mean, what do we teach them? They come to learn, not to be taught. And they learn to be the artists they know they can be.'

'So you don't teach them anything?'

'We give them space. We give them the chance to find them-selves. We let them think about how to express themselves.'

'Dr. Truss,' said the baroness, 'children come to you from school hoping to create. Your job is to give them the skills that enable them to find themselves. Do you teach them to draw?'

'I told you, it's about learning, not teaching.'

'I do beg your pardon. Do you make available to them some-one from whom they can learn to draw?'

'We don't do that kind of thing any more. Drawing is a craft. Not an art.'

'Would that apply to painting? Or sculpting?'

'Of course. If people want to be craftspeople, let them go to craft classes in a technical college. If they wish to be artists, let them come to me.'

'So let me get this clear, Dr. Truss. Young people arrive at your establishment wanting to be artists and mostly not knowing how to draw or paint because their schools have given up on such old-fashioned accomplishments. They have no skills, are subsidised by the taxpayer who thinks they're there to acquire some, yet you teach them nothing because you despise the basic skills that no decent artist can do without.'

'We give them space, Lady Troutbeck. We give them space to fly with their inner selves.'

'Very well, Dr. Truss. Let's look at it from another perspective. Give me an example of how a school like yours produces someone you regard as a great artist.' She paused for a second. 'Let me be specific. I know he didn't go to your college, but tell me what Damien Hirst—whom you have described as an artist of the first rank—*learned* at Goldsmith's College. I know he genuinely wanted to be an artist, despite scoring an E in his 'A' level, he rather amazingly got to art school, he probably wanted to learn to do a bit of drawing and painting, but they were not on offer. What was there for him? Or was he entirely self-made and could have done just as well without art college.'

The baroness would later brag to her friends of how she had set the sap up for this and how, like a low-hung fruit, he fell into her basket.

'Ah, Damien,' he said. 'He has genius, of course, but he would be the first to explain that without Goldsmith's College, which I'm not ashamed to say led the way for the rest of us, he would not be what he is today.'

'And his inspiration was?' asked the presenter.

'Michael Craig-Martin, his tutor.'

'From whom he learned?'

'The essence of conceptual art,' said Truss, reverentially. 'Michael provided the revelatory moment that released Damien from the constraints that glorified draughtsmen would have imposed on him—through his incomparable articulation of neo-conceptualism.'

'Which is?'

Truss laughed. 'You don't even know that? It's the insight that anything can be a work of art.'

'We're short of time, Dr. Truss,' said the presenter. 'Please give us the revelatory moment.'

'Years before Damien became his student, Martin had exhibited what Damien later explained as 'the greatest piece of conceptual sculpture' that he just couldn't get out of his head.' Truss bent his head for a reverential moment. 'You can't imagine how dramatic it was. High on a wall in an empty gallery, Michael installed a glass half-full of water on a small shelf attached to a wall. He called it *An Oak Tree.* In an accompanying leaflet, he asked himself if it was just a case of the emperor's new clothes, but then explained that this was not a glass of water, but "a full-grown oak tree." He had changed it into an oak tree.'

'But he hadn't,' observed the baroness mildly.

'You understand nothing,' said Truss. 'As Sir Nick Serota himself pointed out, appreciating all art requires an act of faith comparable to believing that in transubstantiation, bread and wine become the body and blood of Christ.'

'But you're an atheist,' said the baroness.

'Yes.'

'So you don't even believe in Jesus, let alone in transubstantiation.'

'That's different,' said Truss. 'That's not art.'

'Nor, apparently,' said the baroness, looking at the producer making a ten-second gesture towards the fascinated presenter, 'is anything we taxpayers would wish to pay you to impart to the young art.' She slowed down her delivery. 'Michael Craig-Martin was a trustee of the Tate when Tate Britain filled a room with his talentless scribbles and vacuous conceits. You betray your students, Dr. Truss. You betray us. And, like Sir Nicholas Serota, who indulges you all, you betray art.'

◇◇◇

The baroness woke up, peered into the darkness, put two fingers in her mouth and emitted an ear-splitting whistle. Almost instantly, the neon lights came on. 'Thank you,' she said, with exaggerated politeness. 'Now would breakfast run to coffee and something decent to eat?'

'Coffee, yes. And bread.'

'Eggs?'

'If you promise you won't sing.'

'I promise.'

'Then you can have an egg. One.'

'How were you thinking of cooking it?'

'You wait.'

The baroness allowed herself to fall into a reverie about eggs. She remembered the perfect scrambled eggs she had had on Sarkovsky's yacht, and the excellent Eggs Benedict she had had at the Wolseley with Robert Amiss a few weeks previously, as they prepared themselves for their expedition to Tat Modern. What would Robert be thinking now? Or Mary Lou? Or St. Martha's? Or Myles, if he had heard? If she could make no sense of it, how could they? 'Stop it, old girl,' she said to herself. 'That way madness lies. As Kai Lung said, "When struck by a thunderbolt it is unnecessary to consult the Book of Dates as to the precise meaning of the omen." For now, just survive. One day at a time. One foot in front of the other.'

Her custodian spoke, and they went through the bathroom, lights-out, business with the door, and lights-on routine. The coffee was instant, but at least it was strong. The egg was hardboiled and without salt. And the bread had no butter. But it was food, and the baroness was grateful for it. Having returned her mug and the eggshells, she had to fight off a perverse urge to break into 'Oh, what a beautiful morning,' but suppressed it on the grounds that her lifeline was the tenuous deal with her mysterious provider. Telling herself that she might at some juncture have to make a run for it, she forced herself instead to do a few exercises that did not look too ridiculous and lay back on the bed and decided to recite Shakespearean soliloquies. As an intellectual exercise, she tried to take the plays in alphabetical order. She couldn't remember a single line from *All's Well That Ends Well*, Anthony and Cleopatra yielded only the dismaying 'All is lost!/This foul Egyptian hath betrayed me,' but *As You Like It* was a winner.

Although of a cheerful disposition herself, the baroness had always enjoyed the melancholy Jacques' 'All the world's a stage,/ And all the men and women merely players'. On this occasion, though, while she maintained her spirits for most of the six ages of man, she could hardly bear to get through the seventh, and she momentarily feared she might cry as she finished with: 'Last scene of all,/That ends this strange eventful history,/Is second childishness and mere oblivion,/Sans teeth, sans eyes, sans taste, sans everything.' This would be a hell of a way for everything to end. In or out of this room.

Although not much given to worry or pointless speculation, she couldn't fight off the feeling that whatever Sarkovsky had in mind, it was unlikely to be kind. After all, in Myles' call from Iraq the day before she was kidnapped, hadn't he asked if she'd heard any more from 'that psycho'? He was calling him that, it emerged, because of well-founded rumours he'd heard about the methods he used in settling some personal grudges. She had assured him gaily that Sarkovsky had not reappeared and could be forgotten about and had laughed it off when he told her to be careful.

The baroness allowed her imagination some free rein. Maybe the bastard meant to keep her in this room until she died like the captive in John Fowles' *The Collector*. She then had the even worse memory of the horrible things done to the kidnapped hero in the film of Stephen King's *Misery*.

At this she decided to get a grip, shook her head vigorously and wondered once again what day it was. Clearly she'd been drugged when captured on Wednesday evening; there was no natural light and her watch had been removed, so she had no idea how long she'd been in this room. Would the police by now be taking her disappearance seriously? Would there be any media interest? She recalled uncomfortably that in the past, when involved in *causes célèbres* that had catapulted her temporarily onto front pages, she had merely a walk-on part: other people's corpses had taken centre stage. She hoped that this time any new notoriety she might achieve would not involve her being murdered.

With the help of a small army of police wrenched from other enquiries, Milton was able within twelve hours to piece together the last known movements of all the disappeared. Like the baroness, Hortense Wilde, Gavin Truss, and Anastasia Holliday had gone missing with their cars; like Fortune and Pringle, Herblock and Marilyn Falucci Lamont had last been seen together hailing taxis. Jake Thorogood, it seemed certain, had been pushed into a car outside his own front door. They had all disappeared within a twenty-four-hour period between Thursday and Friday evenings.

Every few hours Milton had to emerge from the Yard to be snapped by a hundred cameras and give a report to an hysterical mob of reporters demanding to know what he thought had happened, who was responsible, had there been a ransom demand, when he expected to find the missing dignitaries, what was taking so long, and what was being done to protect the other likely victims. Inside were teams of police dealing with equally hysterical enquiries from luminaries of the art establishment who were cowering in their offices and homes demanding police protection.

'We are doing everything we can,' Milton told the media in his best stiff police manner, 'but our resources are limited and our priority must be the missing. We suggest that anyone who fears they might be a target should take obvious precautions. Keep your doors locked and don't open them unless you know who's outside. Travel only in groups. And, yes, I'm sure the general public will be quite safe visiting museums and art galleries. Now, if you'll excuse me, I must go back to work.'

Mary Lou rang Amiss first thing on Friday morning. 'I'm in a state. Are you in a state?'

'Sure am.'

'I know our old girl's been in danger before, but this seems much worse.'

'Certainly does.'

'Can you write?'

'Nope. Can you broadcast?'

'I have to. But it's hard.'

'How do you think Ellis is?'

'Knackered. How's Rachel?'

'Well, obviously she's less upset about Jack than you and I would be, but she's sharing in the general gloom. Plus, school is driving her mad.'

'She told me that dreadful story about wanting to take the kids to see some art. Now I know this isn't important at the moment, but it occurred to me this morning that maybe I could give her some support.'

'Yes, please.'

'Worrying about Jack's got me guilt-ridden about not being enough of a warrior for decent values. Do you think it would help if I offered to do my celeb number and come and talk to her class about art? We could show them pictures and talk about great art being cool and I could do my black role-model bit.'

'I think even her headmaster would have a problem killing off that idea, Mary Lou. You're a star, in more ways than one. Send her an email: it'll be a tiny light in the encircling darkness.'

'Oh, good. Now, as Jack would persist in saying improbably, "I must fly."'

◇◇◇

Amiss spent the whole morning reading newspapers and blogs and watching news channels. An alien doing the same would have concluded that on this strange planet nothing mattered but the art world and its denizens, for those who control rolling news seem incapable of focusing on more than one story at a time. The weather was cold and wet, but unfortunate reporters were interviewed outside galleries under dripping umbrellas trying to talk up any evidence of fear or panic they'd uncovered. Photographs of the missing abounded, many showing them socialising with each other in Venice, Vienna, Paris, New York, LA and London and various other playgrounds, which caused the more perceptive viewers to spot that this was indeed an incestuous and opulent world that had little to do with traditional notions of artists starving in garrets.

Of course the media were disappointed that the kidnapper hadn't got hold of a Grade I art celebrity. 'WILL IT BE DAMIEN OR TRACEY NEXT?' wondered one headline hopefully. 'TERROR OF THE MUSEUM BOSSES' trumpeted another, running a photograph of Sir Nicholas Serota looking particularly thin and drawn. 'NIGELLA'S HUSBAND IN HIDING' screamed a third, reporting breathlessly that Charles Saatchi—a man so reclusive he avoided even his own parties—had not been seen for at least a week. Excited by the loss of Herblock and Marilyn Falucci Lamont, and having heard that Jeff Koons was in Europe, the American press were similarly optimistic that he might yet be snatched.

Pooley had had a difficult conversation with Anastasia Holliday's parents in Australia. After the initial shock, there had been an outpouring from her mother about how her lovely girl had fallen into bad company and why it was a tragedy she had abandoned surf for shit—at least, that was what Pooley uncomfortably thought she said. Should they immediately fly to London? Optimism said no, pessimism said yes, cautious policeman said why not give it another day before deciding.

The most recent boyfriend had agreed to come to the Yard, where Pooley had interviewed him briefly. 'Look,' he said, 'We're both from Oz, but I hardly know Annie. But great bird, great body, lol and all that. As for the art, if you ask me, she's been taking the piss and milking those dipsticks for all she could get.'

Closer questioning elicited the information that Anastasia thought Fortune and Pringle wankers and that he'd never heard her speak of any of the other missing people. He added helpfully that she had confided in him that she was running short of another fucking thing to do with anything that emerged from her body, but that she'd said hopefully that while she'd exhausted piss, shit, and everything else that came out of her clacker, maybe there was still some mileage in sweat and chunder if she could work out how to produce them without too much effort.'

'Chunder?'

'Vomit.'

Pooley, who despite years as a policeman had never succeeded in sloughing off all inhibitions, hid his revulsion, thanked him profusely, promised to do everything he could to find Anastasia and to report back tomorrow, and rushed back to his office to investigate an intriguing message. It was ten minutes later when he pressed 'Print,' waited impatiently, grabbed the pages, and raced to Milton's office. 'There's another. At least I think he's another, even though he's a hedge fund manager.'

Milton looked exhausted. 'What do you mean, "I think he's another, even though he's a hedge fund manager"?'

Pooley was excited. 'I mean other people didn't make the link. He'd been missing a few days but I Googled him and saw he'd been buying a lot of very expensive art. Look. There he is: Charlie Briggs. Snapped at a Sotheby's art auction with a model.'

Milton scanned the pages. 'He paid £5 million for what?'

'A Fantona. Lucio Fantona. Look. That's it.'

There was a pause. 'He paid £5 mill for a plain canvas with a slash in the middle.'

'He did.'

'With cretins like that running our financial affairs,' said Milton heavily, 'it's no wonder we're in the state we're in.'

Pooley was almost dancing with impatience. 'Shouldn't we add him to our investigation? He was also last seen hailing a taxi.'

'When?'

'Thursday evening. The security man at his office said he'd left around half nine.'

'If we do, how many's that? Ten?'

Pooley counted them on his fingers. 'Jack, Sir Henry Fortune, Jason Pringle, Anastasia Holliday, Hortense Wilde, Jake Thorogood, Chester Herblock, Marilyn Falucci Lamont, Gavin Truss, and now Charlie Briggs. Yes, ten.'

'I'd better go and tell the AC we've reached a nice round number. That might stop him going on about coincidence. After that we try to find out what connections there are between the missing and Sarkovsky. At this stage, the preliminary interviews are down to you and me. I don't trust anyone else.'

Amiss' afternoon went the way of his morning. Hour by hour, he watched and read every aspect of the lives of the missing being picked over. A sombre tone was adopted by most commentators, who concentrated on what the world owed these people of talent and discernment, with the occasional dissenter opining that they were opportunists who had made fortunes out of endorsing, creating, or buying rubbish. Innumerable celebrities from the art world shared their grief and pain at the fate that had befallen their beloved friends. The social media, on the other hand, were dominated by gossip and rumour and sick jokes and sniggers about sex, drugs, and rock-and-roll.

Late afternoon, the news that Charlie Briggs was thought to be the tenth victim of the same kidnapper cheered everyone up no end, as it enabled them to begin speculating about the safety of every modern-art collector in London. It was a bonus that he was young and good-looking and frenzied attempts were made to link him with Anastasia Holliday, clips of whose frank accounts of what she did with her orifices and her bodily fluids were being held until after the nine o'clock watershed. For now, they were majoring on shots of her falling out of nightclubs.

What confused everyone was where the baroness came into it. In her speech to the House of Lords about contemporary culture, she had trashed the critics and dealers and curators and art schools for being part of a vast liberal conspiracy to destroy everything that made art great and make fortunes along the way. And there were a couple of clips of her being rude on news programmes that made riveting viewing. One tabloid christened her 'Baroness Battle-Axe.' This gave rise to speculation that she was the kidnapper, a suspicion the assistant commissioner was beginning to share.

The sane took the view that she was an unlikely possessor of a paramilitary wing, but as stories came out about her involvement in high-profile murder cases in Cambridge and London, a significant proportion of those following the story on twitter decided there was no smoke without fire and that she could be some kind of secret agent, except there was no consensus on whom she might be working for.

None of St. Martha's staff was prepared to be interviewed, but the desperate hacks roaming its grounds found a few students who couldn't keep their mouths shut. 'The mistress is, like, cool,' was the quote most of the media ran with. A few dusty peers emerged from the Lords to say pompous things about the baroness being a fine woman known for her integrity and her eloquence. A BBC producer who had discovered Amiss had been a close associate of the baroness in several of her better-known adventures rang to beg him for an interview.

'It would,' he said primly, 'be inappropriate,' and ended the call before the man had the wit to ask him why. The truth was that by now Amiss was so terrified for her that he didn't trust himself to keep his composure in public.

Chapter Six

It was mid-afternoon before Milton was finally put through to Mrs. Chester Herblock in her Manhattan home. She sounded hyper. 'Hey, they say you're an English policeman, right?'

'I am.'

'So what do I call you, Mr. Policeman? Over here everyone's "Officer."'

'That'll do fine, Mrs. Herblock.'

'So what can I do for you, Officer?'

'It's to do with your husband's disappearance.'

'His what?'

'Oh, I do apologise. I assumed you'd been told by the NYPD. It was their job.'

'I've haven't been around to be told anything, Officer.' She giggled. 'I've been holed up with a friend and we haven't been taking calls. Only just got home. Chester's hardly ever here anyway, so who'd know he was missing.'

'I'm afraid he hasn't been seen for three days and no one has any idea where he is.'

'Don't you worry, Officer,' she said happily. 'He'll be off with that Lamont bitch. In case you don't know what I'm talking about, my husband is serially unfaithful with bitches of one kind or another, beautiful or sexy or rich. This one's called Mar-il-yn Fal-ucc-i La-mont. I've been expecting him any day now to tell me she's going to be my replacement. Do you know about replacements in my world, Officer?'

'I can't say that I do, Mrs. Herblock. Indeed I don't really know what your world is.'

'It's the cosmopolitan art world, Officer, in which people like my husband drift around arty places from Bel Air to Buenos Aires networking and making a fortune in collusion with dealers and curators to persuade ignorant rich people to waste their money on worthless trash. They also trade up in wives according to their beauty or their money or their performance in bed. I'm the sexy third Mrs. Herblock and I signed a pre-nup. Chester's had his fun and now he's thinking of his future.' She laughed again. 'Poor Chester. He finds being only a multi-millionaire a bit constricting. It's time for me to make way for a billionairess.' She paused. 'That's Lamont,' she said helpfully. 'Lucky woman. She was married to an elderly billionaire who croaked while she was still young enough to enjoy the legacy.'

'Oh,' said Milton, lacking anything else to say.

'So what do you wanna know, Officer?'

Milton pulled himself together. 'There is reason to believe that several people connected with the art world have been kidnapped, Mrs. Herblock, including your husband.'

'What about the rich bitch?'

'She's disappeared...that is, Mrs. Lamont has gone missing too.'

'They were screwing at the Dorchester, right?'

'They were both staying in the Dorchester, Mrs. Herblock.'

'In the same suite?'

'No.'

'Next door?'

'I think so.'

'Of course. After all, money's no object.'

'But please, Mrs. Herblock, my job is to find them. Is there anything you can tell me that would help?'

'Nope. I haven't heard from him for days, but that's nothing new. Off with the old, on with the new, that's Chester Herblock, whether he's dealing with wives or art. But one way or the other, money will be involved. Plenty of it.'

◇◇◇

'Mrs. Herblock had met Sir Henry Fortune at some art event,' said Milton to Pooley. 'She described him as an asshole. She'd also heard of Jason Pringle as someone Herblock occasionally did business with and she heard him mention Anastasia Holliday as a hot new talent.

'"I looked her up," she said, "and saw that even if she didn't seem to have any talent, she was certainly hot, so it was no surprise Chester was taking an interest."

'When I got her to focus on Oleg Sarkovsky, she remembered him vaguely as the guy Herblock told her was a real sap, that he could shovel any shit off on to him and make a bomb. Then she began to laugh. Apparently he'd been literally successful with shit. Although it was gold-plated. Someone called Terence something-or-other.'

'Rings a bell. But did she have anything useful otherwise?'

'No. But at least we're clear there was a Sarkovsky connection. Herblock's PA was more helpful. She seemed rather more bothered about his disappearance than was his wife and told me he'd made a lot out of Sarkovsky even though Sarkovsky drove a hard bargain. She reckons he'd have earned several million in commissions.'

Pooley gulped. 'Several million? Sarkovsky must have been buying hundreds of millions worth.'

'And some of it he was buying from Herblock's bit on the side.'

'Marilyn?'

'Yes. Apparently Sarkovsky bought about $150 million's worth of conceptual art off her last year on Herblock's recommendation. Herblock got ten percent.'

'So it's in his interests that prices be high rather than low?'

'It certainly is, Ellis. And no, I don't understand it either. Anything from your end?'

'Nothing, except that Sarkovsky had some slightly fraught dealings with Pringle and Thorogood.'

'In their capacities as dealer and art critic?'

'Yes.'

'This is all ludicrously incestuous.'

'This world is. Apparently although Thorogood was an art critic and innocents like us might think he should be independent, he acted as a kind of authenticator for dealers. Well, for Pringle, anyway.'

'I don't know why we find this kind of thing surprising,' said Milton gloomily. 'I saw a TV programme recently that told me that in the States academic economists were happy to earn a packet from sitting on the boards of companies they wrote about. So what did Thorogood do for Pringle that involved Sarkovsky?'

'According to Allegra from Pringle's gallery, there was some sort of row about graffiti art. Pringle sold Sarkovsky what he thought was a genuine Banksy.'

'Banksy? That graffiti artist who stencils rats and monkeys onto buildings? How can you sell them?'

'It's complicated. Pringle sold Sarkovsky a seaside hut with a stencilled dangling man that was supposed to be a Banksy, but though Thorogood said he agreed with Pringle that it was the genuine article, other critics thought it was a fake and, anyway, it turned out to be a protected hut that couldn't be removed from its location. Sarkovsky wanted his money back, but Pringle was dragging it out and trying to make him take payment in kind. Apparently, he was offering other less well-known graffiti artists, but Sarkovsky was having none of it. It was the big brand names or nothing for him. Allegra said Sarkovsky was very fierce and shouted a lot over the phone.

'Then I talked to Thorogood's girlfriend. She's relatively new, but she remembered he'd been a bit shaken by some Russian threatening to have him shot. Obviously, Thorogood didn't think he meant it, but he was a bit scared.'

'Is that it?' asked Milton.

'No. I talked to Sir Henry Fortune's PA as well. She said rather loftily that while he had never heard of Sarkovsky, Sir Henry was a very famous man who would have been known and respected by everyone in the art world.'

Pooley looked at his watch. 'I need to go. I'm on my way now to see Charlie Briggs' sister and then Gavin Truss' wife.'

'And I've got a number for Marilyn Falucci Lamont's next-of-kin. The AC's out this afternoon but I'm to see him at six. Maybe by then we'll have enough connections made to force the stubborn bastard to take Sarkovsky seriously.'

It was Charlie Briggs' sister Brenda, who'd been staying with him for a few days, who'd reported him missing. Pooley went to the Docklands penthouse to interview her.

'Sorry about this,' she said in a strong Yorkshire accent, as she ushered him towards a sofa. 'It's a bit depressing.'

Pooley looked around curiously. The room had magnificent views across the Thames, but inside was cheerlessly minimalist. 'It needed a woman's touch,' she said. 'All Charlie did was buy whatever 'e were told to buy by whoever were ordering him round. You wouldn't believe the rubbish 'e came home with. Look at that.' She pointed at a canvas leaning against a wall.

'May I look at it?' asked Pooley and went over and turned it round.

'That looks like a vandalised canvas to me,' she said. 'But having seen some of the stuff 'e's paid a fortune for, it's probably worth a bomb so I'd better not throw it out.'

'It's by a famous artist called Lucio Fantona, Ms Briggs, and I think it's worth a few million.'

'Not to me it isn't. Bluddy rubbish.' She sat down on a nearby sofa and he joined her. 'For fuck's sake,' she said, 'what does our Charlie know about art? 'E's only showing off because he thinks 'e has to. 'E don't know nothin' about culture. We never had no money and we wasn't educated neither. 'E's out of his depth, poor lamb.'

'He's been buying a lot of art, M. Briggs,' said Pooley.

'Stop this Ms. Briggs rubbish, will yah? I'm Bren. Brenda Briggs. Known to everyone as Bren. I'm the thick one. Charlie's the brains.'

She stopped and considered that statement. 'Well, the brains when it comes to making money. Charlie's a bit short of brains when it comes to spending it, if you ask me. Krug and girls and now stupid art by people who can't draw or paint.' She looked Pooley in the eyes. 'E'll be OK, Charlie, won't 'e?'

'I very much hope so, Ms. Briggs.' He caught her glare. 'Sorry, Bren. But we need all the information we can get. I know nothing about your brother except that he makes a fortune in financial services and that he collects art. And, as I've explained, it's the art that seems to be linking the people who've disappeared. Please tell me anything you know. What, for instance, was... is...Charlie like with money?'

'I noticed that "was" turning into "is,", Inspector Pooley. Or can I call you something 'uman?'

'Ellis.'

'Ellis? Never 'eard of Ellis. Sounds as posh as your accent.'

Pooley, who had put long hours into trying to modify his Etonian vowels, winced. 'It's a family name from way back. Sort of religious. A bit Welsh.'

'OK. Like Charlie's named after Granddad. Now why did you say "was"?'

'No reason. It's just that we're a bit frantic trying to find out what all these people were doing before they disappeared so I put them in the past tense. I think they've been kidnapped. I've no reason to think anything worse.'

She put her head on one side, circled her thumbs around each other and said, 'OK. I hope you mean that.

'Now you asked about money, and I can see why, because we'd never 'ave thought Charlie would be rich. 'E were crap at everything at school apart from the maths, where 'e were brilliant, so 'e managed to get to uni. A first for our family.'

'He sounds like one of those geniuses who set up Google or Facebook.'

'You've got it. One of those...what do they call them these days? Sort of autistic lite?'

'Aspergers?'

'That's it. Charlie weren't too good at understanding people, but he certainly understood...' She looked fearfully at Pooley. 'Now you've got *me* talking about him like he were dead.'

'It's OK, Bren. We're talking about his life before now.'

'OK, Ellis. Charlie understood figures and then 'e understood computers and they and 'im were supposed to understand how the world worked. And the world were all about money, and Charlie did things on the computer and 'is firm turned them into money. And 'e got huge money. And 'uge bonuses. And then 'e were given a bit of the company and 'e made even more.'

'What did he do with it?'

''E hadn't no interest in money. 'E'd have given it all away. Our parents wouldn't move, but 'e bought their council 'ouse for them and gave them as much as they'd take. Same with me. Bought me a nice 'ouse and my nail business and I'm doing fine. Me and my 'usband, we don't want nothing more.

'Charlie would have given most of it to charity but 'e had to do the flashy things that made the crazies 'e worked with respect him. Otherwise they'd have bullied 'im even more like they did when 'e was at school. It's all big dick stuff in that world.' She adopted a child's voice: '"Yah, boo, sucks. I wasted more money than you did."'

From further questioning it emerged that Briggs had no steady girlfriend, few friends, and that left to himself his idea of relaxation was to play computer games. But being emotionally reliant on a few of his colleagues who were conspicuous consumers he went out with them for extravagant evenings with expensive girls. Not having any desire for fast cars or yachts or travel, buying art seemed to be the easiest and quickest way to placate his self-appointed advisers.

'Did he know a Russian called Oleg Sarkovsky?'

'Never heard of 'im.'

'Or a favourite art dealer? Or did 'e go to auctions?'

'There was someone advised him. What was his name? Jason summat.'

'Pringle.'

'That's it. 'E said 'e were very learned. And I know they went to auctions, because Charlie said 'e enjoyed bidding. Said it gave 'im a buzz.'

'Thank you, Bren. I was going to ask if I could send in a team to search the apartment for anything that might be useful, but seeing there's so little here, if it's OK with you I'll do it myself now. Won't take long.'

'Anything that'll help get Charlie back.'

All that Pooley could find that was remotely of interest were a few sale catalogues from major London auction houses with scribbles on them. He said goodbye to Bren Briggs and took them away with him.

Mrs. Gavin Truss was pretty, but dishevelled, weary, and depressed. Her toddlers were getting her down. In her chaotic house in Acton, with two small boys running wildly from room to room in screaming pursuit of each other, she explained that she hadn't got alarmed until Friday morning, since Gavin often stayed out without telling her. 'Why would anyone kidnap him? He's probably gone off with someone for the weekend.'

Then, in response to Pooley's sympathetic but probing questioning, she burst into tears and said Truss was 'a serial shagger,' she was his third wife, he was thirty-four years older than her, she'd been his awestruck student, and she'd been a moron to fall for him.

She'd never heard of Sarkovsky, she'd known Fortune and Pringle vaguely from the days when Truss used to take her out, and she'd had a few dreary incomprehensible lectures from Hortense Wilde. 'Stuck-up bitch,' she said. 'Always trashing everything I liked.'

There were thudding sounds and roars from the next room. She ran out, separated the combatants, calmed them down, and switched on the cartoon channel for them. 'Would you like coffee?' she asked when she came back.

'No thanks. I'm fine.'

He could see her relief.

'What did you think of your husband's college, Mrs. Truss?'

'I was a nineteen-year-old from Hartlepool and easily impressed in the beginning. Gavin spotted me and took me to exciting events and I was ever so flattered. But it was all pretty crappy, really, when I think back. They didn't teach you anything except how to sneer at old art and drool over the new stuff. I was secretly relieved to drop out at the end of the first year when I fell pregnant with the twins. I thought it would be romantic to be with Gavin and our babies but it hasn't turned out like that. We bore him, and I'm lonely.'

She waved at the scribbles that defaced the lower section of the walls. 'My boys are conceptual artists,' she said. 'I've named these *Dying Very Very Slowly from a Loveless Marriage*.'

'I haven't fully got to grips with Gavin Truss and Hortense Wilde, Jim, but I've see Mrs. Truss and talked to Gervase Wilde over the phone and neither has heard of Sarkovsky. Neither had Truss' deputy. Truss and Wilde are old pals, though, and Wilde's been a professor at Truss' college for years. I read the lists of the missing out to them and it's clear they knew several of them. I've ticked them off: here's a copy.'

'Thanks, Ellis,' said Milton. 'I didn't do much better with finding out about the Lamont woman. Her daughter was cagey, and said she knew she was friends with Herblock but had no information at all about her London contacts. But then she added that considering Mom spent half her life gadding about Europe at art fairs and auctions, she probably knew anyone worth knowing. "It's like the fashion world," she said. "The same people turn up everywhere deciding what everyone else should think." I don't think she's that fond of her mother.'

He looked at his watch. 'I've got to have another press conference now. You'd better get home. You've had hardly any sleep for days.'

'Neither have you.'

'True. But I can't get away until I've seen the AC and you've got a wife who needs to see you.'

'Mary Lou's working tonight. I've an invitation to eat with Robert and Rachel. Will you call when you've seen the AC?'

'Will do. Tell Robert I'm sure Jack's all right.' He picked up his jacket. 'Why did I say that? I'm not, so don't.'

An hour later, as Milton was pleading with the AC to be allowed to put a surveillance team on to Sarkovsky, the baroness heard his voice: 'You go out room now.'

'Oh, good. I'm going home, am I?'

'You think that you stupid. You meet others.'

The baroness quashed a momentary dread that Sarkovsky might have kidnapped the staff of St. Martha's or her close friends, and said nothing. She put on the jacket of her suit of heathery tweed over her grubby purple shirt and followed instructions, first, to wait in the bathroom, and second to leave it, put on the blindfold now waiting for her on her bed, then turn and face the inner wall. She tried to work out why—since she knew Sarkovsky was the kidnapper—it mattered to him that she didn't see where she was going, but there seemed no logical explanation except that he wanted her further disorientated. The door opened, Sarkovsky barked an order, and a rather sweaty hand grasped her arm and the voice of her regular captor said, 'Come with me.'

She followed obediently, irritated that she had failed in her attempt to rig the blindfold so she could see something. She was in the open air, it was cold, and she was on rough ground. A door was opened, she was pushed through it, and the voice said, 'Take it off in two minutes and walk down the stairs. There's no way out here.'

The lights were so bright when she took the blindfold off that she was initially completely disorientated. She blinked steadily until she was able to take in properly the bizarre grandeur that surrounded her. The curved staircase was carpeted in red, the walls were mirrored, and four enormous chandeliers dangled from the gilded ceiling. 'Crikey,' said the baroness, as she put her hand on the gilt balustrade and began the descent. At the bottom of the stairs there was a large, red door, which required so much strength to open that she had to hurl herself at it.

The enormous room that was revealed was lined with large glass tanks and steel, glass-fronted cabinets. There was a noxious smell of rotten meat. To her right, beside the door, was a glass tank about fourteen feet long and six feet high. In one half was a rotting cow's head and an electric insect killer; along with maggots, flies were feeding on the one and dying on the other. The other half contained a large white box from which flies emerged and found their way through holes in the partition.

She walked down the centre of the room and saw that the cabinets lining the walls to the left contained an eclectic and gruesome array of objects that included pliers, an axe, saw, noose, club and spear, crucifixes, bandages, and rosaries—some of them spattered with what looked like blood. The same substance was spattered over the outside of the cabinet, and emanated a cloying smell which was only slightly less disgusting that that by the door. To the right were several identical large black canvases. She went over and inspected one of them and saw that the canvas had been blackened by tens of thousands of dead flies: the title was *Cancer Chronicle (Smallpox)*.

At the end of the room was the *pièce de resistance*, a huge perspex box containing five white plastic chairs surrounding a matching table with the remains of a meal on it. In the corner was a barbecue laden with meat. Everything was covered in live flies that entered via a small hole from the other part of the exhibit, where maggots were hatched, and perished on another fly killer.

'Sweet Jesus,' said the baroness. 'I'm in hell with Damien Hirst.'

She explored further. There were three locked doors—red, black, and violet—and a doorless kitchen scribbled over with graffiti and images mainly of rats. A white door led to a bathroom, on the far wall of which was a sketch of a complex piece of machinery, and a shelf on which were a small irregularly-shaped, gold-covered object and a tin. Closer scrutiny revealed that the sketch was called *Cloaca* and the curved object had a tag saying 'Koh?' The label on the tin was in four languages. The baroness passed on the French, German, and Italian and read the English text:

'Artist's Shit
Contents 30 gr net
Freshly preserved
Produced and tinned
in May 1961'

She groaned and left the bathroom.

Having searched high and low, the baroness had to admit to herself that there was no food, but there was champagne in the refrigerator and she found glasses in a cupboard. She opened a bottle, poured herself a generous amount, and returned to the main room and sat on one of the four large pink sofas shaped like a woman's lips. It was very uncomfortable.

After a few minutes, there was a crashing sound at the door. When it opened, it revealed a plump, dishevelled middle-aged, bald man in a dinner jacket. The baroness stood up and crossed to him, holding her hand out. 'Jack Troutbeck.'

'What's going on?' He gave her a perfunctory handshake. 'Why am I here?'

'Search me. I don't know why I'm here either. Who are you?'

'I am Sir Henry Fortune, the international curator.'

'Oh, God.' She sat down again. 'So you are.'

He looked around him and blenched. 'Is this a museum?'

'I have no idea. I've been here only a few minutes.'

'Disgusting smell.' His tone implied it was her fault. 'Is there anything to eat? I'm starving.'

''Fraid not. But there's champagne.'

'What good is that? I tell you I'm starving.'

The baroness shrugged. 'There are calories in wine. Do you want some or not?'

'I suppose so.'

The baroness fetched two bottles from the kitchen along with a few glasses and put them on one of the two low tables that sat between the sofas. Both tables consisted of glass tops supported by the form of a woman. Each wore a basque and long black gloves: one was on her hands and knees; the other was on her back but had cunningly bent her body into a shape than supported the table on her bottom. The baroness had already named them Joleen and Trixie.

Fortune poured himself a glass and sat down opposite her. 'So who are you?'

'I'm a member of the House of Lords and Mistress of St. Martha's.'

'Oh, my God. I know who you are. You're that dreadful philistine.'

'Do you think we know each other well enough to exchange insults yet, Sir Henry?' she enquired icily. 'I think I'd rather be in solitary, but I don't suppose I have an option. Maybe we should make an effort to be civil.' She got up, refilled her glass, and sat down again. 'Have you been here long?'

'I don't know. Maybe a few days. I've been imprisoned in a nasty cell and I've had nothing to eat.'

'How did you get here?'

'I don't know. Last thing I remember is getting into a taxi with a friend.'

'So presumably he's here too.'

'I don't know. This is a nightmare.'

'Unfortunately not,' said the baroness.

Fortune said nothing.

'What do you think of the décor?' she asked.

'I haven't really looked at it.'

'You're in for a treat if your idea of an interior decorator is Damien Hirst. It's a bit on the gloomy side.'

'Damien Hirst is an artist, Madam. It is not his job to cheer anyone up. I have to think about what is here. I don't want to make any rash judgements.' He stalked over to the tank beside the door. 'Is this truly Damien's *A Thousand Years*? I doubt it. He would never sell this audacious yet profound Darwinian masterpiece.'

'Look down the room and you'll see something else by him.'

He strode down the room. '*Let's Eat Outside Today*. It cannot be. It cannot be.'

'Do you recognise what's on the left?'

Fortune's lips went in and out as he ruminated. 'Of course. I've only seen them once. In the White Cube about a decade ago.' He clicked his fingers in frustration. 'What was it called? What *was* it called. Hah! Yes. *Romance in the Age of Uncertainty.*'

'They represent romance?'

'No, no, no. They represent the martyred apostles.'

'Ah, got you. He's showing us the means by which they were martyred. Neat.'

'Yes.'

'And the black canvases?'

'His thirteen *Cancer Chronicles*—smallpox, AIDS, malaria, and so on. But I am sceptical as to their authenticity. Very sceptical.'

'Have you any thoughts on the Mae West sofas?'

'Crude adaptions of Dali's surreal masterpieces.'

'And Trixie and Joleen?'

'What are you talking about?'

The baroness waved at the tables.

'Oh, you mean the Allen Jones sculptures? Which, of course, may or may not be Allen Jones.'

'They're art, are they? I thought they were cast-offs from Hugh Hefner's Playboy Mansion.'

Fortune looked down his nose at her like an Edwardian dowager duchess surveying the shop girl her son wants to marry. He produced a heavy sigh. 'They raise many questions that have been addressed by serious and knowledgeable people: is such forniphilia Freudian, or an ironic comment on sexual objectification and the struggle between the exploited and the exploiting.'

The baroness opened her mouth and closed it again. 'Have a look at the kitchen.'

He came out after a minute. 'The same applies. Of course they look like Banksy, but are they Banksy? That is the question.'

'And our bathroom?'

Fortune disappeared for a couple of minutes. 'How exciting,' he said when he reappeared and threw himself down on the sofa opposite her. 'The same seminal question applies but the Manzoni, at least, would be harder to copy. If all is as it seems, what we have in there are...'

There was a series of thuds at the door. 'If I'm not mistaken, Watson,' said the baroness, 'here is our client now.'

The door crashed open and revealed a skinny, long-haired man in a dinner jacket. 'Jason,' cried Fortune and rushed over to him.

'Oh, Bubbles!' cried Pringle. 'I've had a most ghastly time and they won't give me anything to eat, however I plead. Is there food here?'

He looked around him and screamed. 'Has Damien kidnapped us? Are we an installation?'

'We don't know.'

Pringle looked over at the baroness, who was regarding him with interest. 'Who's she?'

'That bigoted woman who made that dreadful speech in the Lords calling us and Nick Serota and Charles Saatchi and lots of others terrible names.'

'My name is Jack Troutbeck,' said the baroness. 'And you are?'

'Jason Pringle. I'm an art dealer.'

'Indeed you are, Mr. Pringle. Your fame has preceded you.'

'Is there any food?'

'I'm afraid not. But we should remember that hunger strikers have managed to stay alive for more than sixty days, so it's a bit early to make a fuss.'

Fortune and Pringle shot her glances of pure hatred. 'There is champagne, Mr. Pringle. I suggest you have a drink. I further suggest that—although you can be assured that I dislike you both just as much as I'm sure you do me—since we're incarcerated together for God knows how long it might be an idea to try to get on if it's at all possible.'

She rose, filled a glass, and handed it to Pringle with exaggerated courtesy. 'Thank you,' he muttered.

However, leaving her with just Joleen for company, Fortune and Pringle withdrew to the sofa furthest away and began what the baroness described contemptuously to herself as canoodling and caterwauling. After a few minutes, there was another assault on the door and a tall, skinny woman in jeans and a big woolly navy sweater appeared. The baroness looked at her in horror. Fortune and Pringle jumped up and rushed over and embraced her. 'Darling,' they cried in unison.

'Oh, Henry and Jason, how wonderful to see you,' said Hortense Wilde, with a sob. 'Is there anything to eat? What's going on here?'

'It seems to be a remake of *Huis Clos*,' said the baroness. 'Would you care for a drink?'

Chapter Seven

'I thought there couldn't be two Ellis Pooleys,' said the elegant man who got up from behind his desk and came forward, holding out his hand.

Pooley shook it. 'And I thought there were unlikely to be two Adam Eichbergs.'

'Do sit down.' Eichberg waved at an upright leather armchair. 'Coffee?'

'Please.'

While Eichberg was talking to his secretary, Pooley assessed the furniture and the pictures and concluded that his old classmate was doing very well indeed. Eichberg put down the phone, sat in a matching chair, and surveyed Pooley. 'You don't look much different from when we were at school, Ellis. I suppose I shouldn't be surprised that you ended up in the police. I seem to remember that you were mad keen on Sherlock Holmes.'

'And I seem to recollect you preferring art to anything, Adam. I remember those Renaissance reproductions in your study.'

Eichberg laughed. 'So in our case, the boys really were the fathers of the men.'

'Though I'd have expected you to go the art historian route rather than the commercial.'

'Couldn't have done it in the present climate, Ellis. I don't fit in with the orthodoxy of the times. As a curator it would have killed me to buy and extol dross. As an auctioneer, I don't care.

'Anyway, you didn't come here to visit an old school acquaintance. What do you want from me? Is it to do with these extraordinary disappearances?'

'It is. I'm trying to establish various links. And I'm told you were the auctioneer at these sales.' Pooley pushed across three of the catalogues he'd taken from Briggs' flat.

Eichberg threw them a cursory look. 'Yes, indeed. They were most successful.'

Pooley handed him a photograph. 'This is one of the missing people: Charlie Briggs. Do you remember him at any of them?'

'I'm not quite sure. I saw this photo in a newspaper this morning, and thought he seemed vaguely familiar. But that's all.'

'He might have been with Jason Pringle.'

Eichberg snapped his fingers. 'Oh, course. Yes, I remember. He was the one who bought that Fantona.'

'He was indeed. And a few other things.'

There was a tap on the door and a Kate Middleton look-alike came in with a tray. 'Thanks, Jemima. Just leave it.' She smiled a dazzling smile and left in a waft of expensive perfume.

'How do you get Jemimas to lower themselves to make coffee?'

'Come on, Ellis. You must know there's an infinite supply of well-bred young girls with degrees in fine arts who are happy to work for a pittance in places like these.' He pushed a cup of black coffee across the desk. 'Help yourself to milk, sugar, and biscuits.'

'Thanks.'

'Now what do you want to know?'

'If you remember anything of significance about him? Anything that might give a clue as to why he might have an enemy?'

Eichberg frowned. 'In my line of work, discretion is of the essence.'

'As it is in mine, Adam. However, these people are in very real danger. We're desperate for leads.'

'That puts it in perspective. Did you know I'm Jewish? One of the good things about my religion is that it tells me it's OK to break the Sabbath to save a life. So I guess I can break the rules of my ancient auction house for the same reason.'

'I appreciate that, Adam. And I'd be really grateful for anything you could tell me that will help me understand this peculiar world. I'm floundering.'

'I met Briggs with Pringle at a reception where newcomers are fattened up for the market. Briggs seemed a nice bloke but hadn't a clue. Typical ignorant hedgie. Jason Pringle is a shark: Briggs, being ignorant and rich, is typical of his prey. What's more, like so many of these young men who've got rich quick, he's competitive and a gambler. I guess Jason realised early on that he'd do better pointing him at auctions than trying to get him to buy from the gallery.'

'How would Pringle make money that way?'

'By arrangement with the sellers.'

'Can you explain that?'

'Let's suppose I'm an unscrupulous dealer trying to off-load an artwork worth, say, a million, on the open market. I'd like to make more, of course, so I tip off my dodgy friends among art advisers and dealers in the hope that they can deliver a mug or two who'll buy or at least drive up the price. If they do so, they'll get a commission. Pringle was good at providing mugs and Briggs was ideal. He'd no idea what he was bidding for, but was happy to go far above any sensible limit on Pringle's say-so and just for the fun of it.'

'As he did for the Fontana?'

'Yes. He paid a bit over the odds for that. But I was more thinking of the way he bid for that sub-standard Hirst.'

'What's a sub-standard Hirst?'

Eichberg laughed. 'I can see you're not a fan. Nor am I. When I came into this game it was because I loved great art. I've ended up spending much of my time peddling garbage, but I tell myself everyone involved is a consenting adult—curators, dealers, collectors and, indeed, auctioneers. They all want money or prestige or status.'

'And critics and art historians and teachers?'

'Indeed. They're all caught up in this vast confidence trick.'

'So no one can afford to mention that the artist-emperor is naked?'

'You could argue that the artists are the tailors and the rest are the emperors, Ellis. After all, smart artists have learned to exploit the parasites. And good luck to them, I say. I live in hope that one day the entire market for this trash will implode and we can get back to selling exquisite tailoring.'

'You were saying about Briggs.'

'We had a lot with an estimated price of nine hundred K. When we reached that, everyone dropped out except for a telephone bidder and Briggs. Briggs finally quit when the price got to just under three million, and the telephone bidder got it for three.'

'If Briggs was that competitive, why didn't he go to three?'

'I saw Pringle whisper to him as I asked if he'd like to raise his bid. And he shook his head.'

'So what do you think was going on?'

'Briggs is rich. Not mega-rich. It would make sense to let him keep his money for the next time round. Assuming Pringle was getting a cut of that deal, which I'm sure he was, he was essentially taking his winnings and keeping Briggs' money in reserve for another punt another time.'

'Who was the telephone bidder?'

'If I ever knew I don't remember. Hang on a minute. I'll get Jemima onto it. I need to go to her. She'll have the catalogues.'

While he was out of the room, Pooley called the office, got an update reporting no news and no progress, and attended to some emails. After five minutes, Eichberg returned. 'Got it,' he said. 'Fiona, our representative who was manning the phone, remembers the guy well. She said she had a horrible time with him because he was furious that he'd paid so much. And yet, he obviously couldn't bear to lose.'

'And he was?'

'You realise how tricky this is, Ellis. We promise client confidentiality. And I know this man and he wouldn't react well if he knew.'

'I understand, Adam. But there are ten missing people.'

'I know, I know.' Eichberg sighed. 'OK. He was called Oleg Sarkovsky.'

'Yes, I've talked to Sarkovsky, sir,' said Milton. 'It took me ages to get hold of him, but I created merry hell with his people and eventually he called. He says he hasn't seen her since they parted company at the airport weeks ago.'

'Where is he?'

'He claims he's in Moscow, but he could easily be lying. I'm asking MI6 to check if he's there. And we should search his London house now. And get that cell phone traced.'

'Hold on, Jim. Hold on. I don't want to ask favours of Six unless we're sure it's necessary. Don't want to be beholden…'

'But, sir…'

The assistant commissioner took off his reading glasses, folded them neatly and laid them on the desk. 'Look here, Jim, this is an order. Relations with Six are very delicate at the moment and I don't want any boats rocked. The only reason this bloke's a suspect is that Troutbeck talked about him. If you ask me, she's a more likely suspect. From all I hear she had an obsessive hatred for artists.'

By taking a deep breath, Milton succeeded in keeping his temper. 'I can see why you might think that, sir' he said, 'but I've known Lady Troutbeck for some years, and although she's eccentric, she's eminently sane.'

'It can be a small step from eccentricity to insanity,' said the assistant commissioner, with the faux-wisdom that so grated on his juniors.

'She is also someone who has to live on a salary which would not allow her to employ a team of skilled kidnappers.'

'I suppose you're right. Though they make a lot out of expenses in the Lords.'

Milton kept his voice level. 'Which leaves us with ten people missing and only one suspect, sir. We can't ignore that.'

'But we don't want to make any mistakes. According to this…' He put his glasses back on again and looked at the brief, 'as well as his Kensington mansion, Sarkovsky's got homes in the Hamptons and the Antibes, a Scottish shooting lodge, a helicopter, a private plane, and a yacht.' He took off his glasses again, put them on the desk, clasped his hands together and adopted an expression suitable to a primary school teacher explaining there was no Santa Claus. 'If, Jim, and it's a very big if, Sarkovsky's the perpetrator, the victims could be absolutely anywhere. And, if he'd really had it in for them, they'd be at the bottom of the ocean wearing cement shoes.'

'We can't give up, sir. He's the only lead we've got. There are connections between him and almost everyone on the list.'

'There must be thousands of people in the arty world who innocently know many people on that list, Jim.'

'We know he had rows with some of them. And a really bad one with Lady Troutbeck. We've got absolutely nothing else that makes any sense at all.'

'You call this sense?' The assistant commissioner shook his head more in sorrow than anger at Milton's denseness. 'You're seriously suggesting we should bother Six and get a search warrant on the basis that he had a row with that Troutbeck lunatic, who seems to have rows with everyone? Don't think I don't know what she said in the Lords about the Met being full of wimps and appeasers. Anyway, if Sarkovsky hated Troutbeck that much, he could have had her knocked off and dropped down a mine while he was out of the country.'

'But there are the other missing people, sir. And his reputation is terrible.'

'He's got a dodgy reputation and has the occasional business dispute? For fuck's sake, Jim, you know as well as I do that London's full of people with a dodgy reputation. Especially Russians. But they're not mad enough to start mass kidnappings. The odd poisoning, maybe, but not snatching people off the street in broad daylight.'

The assistant commissioner picked up his glasses once more, put them on and bent his head again over the briefing papers. 'The first thing the judge is going to ask is why we think Sarkovsky might have had it in for any of the others.'

'There's speculation that he's lost a lot of money on art and he thought Pringle and Thorogood had pulled a fast one. But my hunch is that we're not involved with someone rational. My sources suggest he's in bad financial trouble and it's probably irrecoverable. He seems to have been in close working relationships with a few unsavoury Arab dictators now dead or deposed. If he's losing everything, he could be looking for a dramatic exit. He acquired the money violently. Why not go down gloriously?'

'That sounds like Ellis Pooley is kite-flying again.'

'Ellis' theory is the only one we've got. People do go mad, and this guy—from all we hear—is a paranoid megalomaniac.'

The assistant commissioner bent over the file again. 'I'll think about it.'

'We've got to do something, sir. Can't we at least put a team on to investigating what other properties he might own?'

'Surely you realise these people have brilliant accountants and lawyers to keep their business affairs under wraps, Jim. We haven't the manpower for this.'

'We can't do nothing, sir. The press are baying for our blood.'

The assistant commissioner adopted his sagacious tone. 'I'm surprised at you, Jim. We can't be jumping to the tune of the reptiles. At least not when we're deciding if we should take on someone of unlimited wealth. I said I'd think about it. And that's what I'll be doing tonight. See you first thing tomorrow.'

Milton could have done with knowing about Martin Conroy, who was sitting at his home computer triumphantly adding another company name to the list he kept in his Oleg Sarkovsky file. As ever, Conroy had worked steadily through the day in his office clearing the urgent files. It was mostly humdrum work, but he never complained. His sequence of bosses in his twenty years in Inland Revenue appreciated him for his competence, reliability, and punctuality. It was a relief to have someone who needed minimal supervision and just got on with things. He was promoted from time to time, but being avowedly uninterested in management, he would never fly as high as his other capabilities could have brought him.

There were two other reasons why he hadn't sought promotion. One was because high office would not have been compatible with his career as an army reservist, the first major outlet for his sense of adventure. Conroy had never wanted to join the army full-time, mainly because, as with the police, there was far too much sitting around being bored. And Jane had made it very clear early on that while she didn't mind him being away for evenings, weekends, and even the odd couple of weeks, she would never agree to being an army wife. She'd become annoyed, though, when he joined the Special Forces Reserve, which required longer and more intensive training.

By the time she stunned him by announcing she had fallen in love with his sister and they had walked off into the sunset, Conroy was set in his ways. He served a few months in Iraq as a member of the clerical support staff and found it both dull and exciting, but he hadn't enjoyed the pain and inconvenience when he took a bullet in his shoulder, and being at the end of his contract, he decided to quit. He kept a few army friendships and attended the odd reunion, but henceforward, he concentrated in his spare time on his second interest, pursuing tax evaders of his choice even when they were none of his business.

His routine was invariable. He arrived at the office at eight and spent precisely seven hours on his allocated work. Since he brought a sandwich with him and ate it at his desk, he was through his work by four, when he turned with eager anticipation to whatever was his current out-of-hours project.

Conroy ran a tight ship and required his staff to run past him not just the tax returns with which they were struggling, but those they had approved. This process not only provided quality control but also occasionally threw up an unexpected and interesting fact that provided the basis for an informal investigation. Conroy didn't just work at the office: if he felt he was venturing into worlds he didn't want to explore on his computer, he would follow up at home, often with the help of a well-placed phone call to an old comrade. And he also believed in occasional on-the-spot spying.

He had first become interested in Oleg Sarkovsky when the approved tax return of his butler, Joseph Taylor, landed in the in-tray. Conroy's latest project had just come to a satisfactory end when he was able to tip-off the Border Agency that a Clapham restaurant—which claimed to have three employees—was operating mostly on the labour of illegal immigrants.

Conroy noticed that Taylor lived in the most expensive part of Kensington, but had a very modest salary, and he wondered why. A check on the electoral roll showed him living there alone, so Conroy spent some time finding the name of its owner, which proved to be a company registered in the British Virgin Islands which had not disclosed the names of the directors.

It took only a couple of hours to identify the owner and occasional resident as Oleg Sarkovsky. Conroy didn't like what he learned from an ex-comrade who was well-informed about Russian oligarchs, so he set himself to find out everything he could about him. By now, he thought he almost had him nailed.

Hortense was in animated and distressed conversation with Fortune and Pringle on their sofa when Gavin Truss arrived, wearing jeans and a t-shirt with the legend: 'That which is cannot be true—Herbert Marcuse.' He took one look at the baroness and screeched like a banshee who was having a particularly bad night. Fortune, Pringle, and Hortense wrapped themselves around him and bore him off to their enclave. By now they had glasses and a couple of bottles standing at the ready on Trixie, so there was no reason for the baroness to proffer drinks. She shrugged, fetched herself another bottle, and a hopeful empty glass, and returned to Joleen and tried to think positive thoughts.

When Jake Thorogood arrived, his torn dressing gown failing to cover his bare shins, she was encouraged that she didn't recognise him, but their exchange of names brought neither of them comfort and he was borne off so fast by Fortune and Pringle that there was no time even for a cursory nod. By now the anti-baroness faction had spread over two sofas, so the occupants had to converse across Trixie. She could hear occasional words like 'bitch,' 'rude,' and 'Neanderthal' which she assumed meant she was under discussion.

She was momentarily cheered when the next entrant was also someone she didn't recognise. He was a dapper man in his fifties, whose expensive haircut, well-fitting tuxedo, and red satin waistcoat seemed to have weathered recent challenges better than the clothes of his fellow captives.

He saw her first, walked over and held out his hand. 'Hey, I'm Chester Herblock.'

'Jack Troutbeck,' she said. But before their handshake was naturally concluded, Fortune and Pringle had swooped once again and hustled him away. Pringle made an attempt to move one of Joleen's sofas, but it proved to be rooted to the floor, so the sofa containing Fortune became full to overflowing.

The next arrival failed to get the door open, and the baroness, being nearest to it, obligingly tugged at the door-handle and revealed a stick-insect in a sable coat over a long, crumpled, dirty, white silk dress and tottering on six-inch gold sandals. Herblock was already there to gather her in his arms, crying, 'Marilyn, darling. We're re-united at last,' and support her back to his group. She was so thin, noted the baroness sourly, that even with her coat on, she made almost no demand on space. Her face was as unlined as that of a fifteen-year-old; the baroness guessed she was in her sixties.

When no one seemed to recognise the dark young man in a pin-stripe suit, pink shirt, matching tie, and Fedora when he tumbled through the door, the baroness hoped she might be in luck, but within seconds Pringle had called 'Charlie' loudly, and identified him to the others as 'a dear friend and the purchaser of a darling Fontana'; he had been clasped to their corporate bosom. Herblock gave him his seat and perched elegantly on Trixie's glass top.

By now the baroness was feeling positively lonely in her splendid isolation, but she was not yet ready to do anything about it. She eavesdropped on the whines about food and the smell and the vying for sympathy, but while she snarled to herself about their having the instincts of a herd of sheep, she had some sneaking sympathy for them. She, at least, was not starving: her last secret meal before leaving her cell had been full of carbohydrates. When, occasionally, someone looked over at her with an expression of mingled disbelief and loathing, she raised her glass in a gesture of good fellowship. And when they looked away again, she put a brave face on it and tried not to think about the immediate future. When there was another commotion at the door, she groaned inwardly. All I need now, she thought, to add to the gaiety of nations, is Sir Nicholas Serota himself.

It proved to be instead an attractive rangy blonde, in skin-tight red jeans, snake-skin boots, and a black top with a neckline that revealed most of her chest. She cast her eye around the room and said: 'Jeez, I don't know about you drongos, but I'm as mad as a cut snake.'

Entranced by the appearance and demeanour of the newcomer, who identified herself as Anastasia Holliday, the baroness decided instantly to make her a friend and ally. After Fortune and Pringle had fallen upon Anastasia with shrieks of joy, and there had been a few minutes for the sharing of recent experiences, the baroness took her by the elbow, detached her from the *melée* and said, 'I'm Jack, Anastasia. And I like Australians. There is only champagne, but here's a glass of it. Come and sit beside me and tell me about yourself.'

To her relief, Anastasia put up no resistance. 'This is a right crockload of shit and no mistake, Jack. I suppose it's a relief that I'm not alone. I've been like a bandicoot on a burned ridge.' She lowered her voice. 'But it's not good news to be locked up with those dipsticks? If I have to be in an asylum, I don't want to be with star fuckers.'

'Aren't some of them your friends?'

'Might have said so few days ago, but I've had plenty of time to think. Being hungry makes you sharper. One think I thunk was that the arty-farties I've been hanging with—some of them are over there—were pseuds and fuckwits and as dry as a dead dingo's donger.'

The baroness raised an eyebrow. 'Weren't some of them instrumental in making you rich and famous?'

'Oh, sure. But just because you've got a good pimp doesn't make you a happy hooker. I'm over being a show pony.'

Everyone jumped as Sarkovsky's voice announced: 'You all here. Now you listen. I Beeg Brother.'

'You Oleg Sarkovsky,' said the baroness.

'Shuddup you. You talk about me, you die. I Beeg Brother. This Beeg Brother house.'

'What's he talking about?' whimpered Fortune.

'I don't know,' said Herbloch.

'Strewth,' said Anastasia. 'Where've you been? Everyone knows about Big Brother. Biggest TV show all over the world.'

'You explain them,' came the instruction.

Crisply, Anastasia explained how people volunteered to shack up together, be spied on around the clock, and win a lot of money.

'You say them eviction consequence of task,' prodded the voice.

'What's the prize?' asked Thorogood hopefully.

'No prize,' said the voice.

'This is illogical,' said the baroness. 'What's our incentive to do these tasks if we all want to be evicted?'

'You evicted, you killed,' said the voice helpfully.

'You cannot be serious,' said Jason Pringle. 'Oh, Bubbles,' he shrieked, throwing himself on Henry Fortune's ample breast.

'I'm sure he's not,' said the baroness gruffly. 'He's just trying to frighten us.'

'It is truth. Now, feeeeerst task. Laidee Troutbeck eat hamburger.'

The baroness' scowl cleared. 'I don't mind that,' she said, 'as long, of course, as it's made of Aberdeen Angus beef. Rump is a possibility, though sirloin is usually preferable. It must have been well-hung. And mind you make sure there's enough fat. And that it's coarsely ground. And, of course, rare. Now with it, I want...'

Though oblivious to the incredulous expressions on the faces surrounding her, she registered the menace in the 'Shuddup and follow instruction' that boomed from the speakers. 'The hamburger McDonald's. Surf Turf. Weeth processed cheese.' He laughed merrily. 'From yesterday.'

'It doesn't matter if it's last year's,' said the baroness bitterly. 'Not being food, it doesn't decompose.'

'And with chocolate meeelkshake. Beeg, beeg, super-size.'

'You cannot be serious, Oleg,' she cried piteously. 'Why would you do that to me?'

'I say you, you name me Oleg, you die. I Beeg Brother. I very serious man. I hear all you say. Anyone talk about Oleg Sarkovsky, Albanians kill him. Hamburger hatch. Kitchen. Eat. Drink.'

'I'm certainly not going to consume such muck,' said the baroness haughtily, grateful that—unlike the others—she wasn't starving. 'I'd rather die.'

'OK. No problem. I happy help.'

'Stuff and nonsense, Ol...Big Brother. You're losing your marbles. You can't bully me.'

'He can kill you,' whispered Pringle, whose normally supercilious expression had long since been replaced by one of abject terror.

'Rubbish,' said the baroness. 'He's having a lark. There's nothing to be worried about.'

'You not eat. No food in house. Never. All very hungry and die.'

'He's bluffing,' said the baroness. She looked at her companions for reassurance and found none.

'Please eat it,' sobbed Pringle.

The baroness looked uncertainly at her companions and saw that Marilyn had begun to cry. Then Anastasia leaned over, clapped her on the thigh and said, 'Think bush-tucker trial.'

'Think what?'

'It's something people do on reality shows to prove they're tough.' The baroness obviously wavered. 'Look, Jack, if I was you I'd stop grizzling and get on with it. We're in the shit and no mistake. Would you rather eat the Macca's or cark it?'

'Cark it?'

'Like he said. Die.' Anastasia made a cutting motion across her throat.

'I'm not sure.'

'It wouldn't be just you,' said Pringle. 'It'd be all of us. We could end up cannibals.'

The baroness ruminated for a moment, turned her head towards the skeletal Pringle and sighed. 'I suppose if you put it that way, there are worse things than a revolting hamburger. None of you looks edible—except possibly Anastasia.'

She heaved herself up and surveyed her companions. 'I want to do this alone.' And assuming an expression so agonised that Marie Antoinette might have considered it over-the-top as she mounted the steps to the guillotine, the baroness gazed neither to right nor left as she marched into the kitchen and opened the hatch.

As there was no door to the kitchen, the nine starving people could not but hear the baroness' loud curses as she chomped and slurped her way through her test. There was little sympathy for her when she emerged from the kitchen complaining that she had never had such a disgusting meal in her life. She marched over to the most visible camera and said, 'I've done it. Now what about food for the others?'

'Feerst you go in Diary Room.'

'What?'

'Red door.'

Had the baroness ever seen Big Brother, she would have been less surprised to find a tiny room furnished only with an enormous purple armchair. 'Seet.'

As she sat down, her eyes flickered over to the door opposite the one through which she'd come.

'You crazy if you think escape. Albanians has machine guns.'

'Nothing could have been further from my thoughts.'

'Now. Orders.'

'For food, do you mean?'

'Shuddup. Orders from me. For you. I give food. Drink. Then you start argument.'

'About what?'

'Art. I want argument. Beeg argument. You make them crazy.'

'Is this just for fun, or is there a deeper reason?'

'You discover, maybe. Now you follow instruction. And not say from me. Go in now, say food here in short time.'

'We're all filthy. Any chance of a change of clothes? And toothbrushes and razors and that kind of thing?'

'Maybe. If I like argument.'

Discretion, concluded the baroness uncharacteristically, was undoubtedly now to be embraced rather than valour. 'OK,' she said. 'Thank you.'

◇◇◇

Akim Zeka had been looking at his watch all afternoon, waiting for the moment when he could stop watching those boring people and get away to Edona. The boss had been very reluctant to let him leave even for a short time, but he needed Akim to be ready to direct proceedings later on, and he had known Akim long enough to know that sexual frustration made him erratic. Sarkovsky wished that this operation could be run by someone calm and effortlessly competent like Taylor, but the butler had made it clear that what he did was to run Sarkovsky's UK establishments and that he wanted no involvement in anything that might be less than respectable. 'I realise that with your business interests you need tough people to protect you, sir,' he told his boss. 'But I want nothing to do with those uncouth Albanians.'

Which left Sarkovsky stuck with Akim Zeka and his family to do his dirty work. They were effective enough, their way, and he was pleased with their complete absence of scruples in the way they protected his property and dealt with a few of his troublesome rivals. The preparations and the kidnappings had gone well, even if they had failed with Saachi and Serota.

'You not forget, Akim. Tonight important.'

'Everything ready. Dritan in charge. I will be back in two hours. All will go very well.'

'No drink?'

'No drink. I go now, Boss. Be back soon.' Akim rushed upstairs and out of the building, jumped into his car and drove as fast as he could to the family brothel in Camden Town.

Chapter Eight

The food was mostly cold meat, cheese, and bread, but it came soon and was plentiful and everyone except the baroness fell on it. Still feeling slightly nauseous, she picked at a few bits of cheese, but concentrated on the accompanying reasonably decent claret. Having remembered uneasily that she had once held forth to Sarkovsky on the evils of Surf 'n Turf, the baroness decided that since he seemed to have gone mad, in the foreseeable future it might be prudent to keep her mouth shut about what she didn't like. She also resolved to obey instructions with the minimum of fuss.

When they had eaten, they were instructed to look in the hatch, where they found ten sports bags with their names on them. Instructions were to change their clothes quickly and throw what they were wearing in the bath. If their spirits lifted slightly at seeing basic toiletries, they fell when they saw their changes of clothing, but there were no protests.

They reconvened in the living room wearing violently-coloured shell-suits that made everyone except Anastasia look ridiculous. They were hardly relaxed, but the tension dissipated slightly as the wine bottles emptied. Even the hostility towards the baroness had somewhat abated. She had, after all, succeeded in her task.

By now inmates were dispersed more evenly on the sofas and conversation was general. They were too scared of Big Brother to discuss what might happen, so they engaged in cosy chit-chat about the cosmopolitan nature of their world. Anastasia, Charlie Briggs, and the baroness, who had had little to do with this glittering scene, had nothing to contribute to the orgy of reminiscence.

Marilyn Falucci Lamont, it emerged, was a legendary patron of contemporary art who gave mega bucks to famous art galleries and museums and had distinguished collections of her own in her various houses. Her diary was constructed around major art events around the world. She had first met Fortune at a Venice Biennale, Pringle in Madrid, and Thorogood in Morocco. Herblock, her long-term adviser, was as peripatetic, flitting around the globe finding new artists for his eager collectors. He had formed relationships with many art colleges, which is how he had come to know and trust Gavin Truss and Hortense Wilde.

The baroness remained silent and listened keenly, but the conversation was too general to give her an opening, so she seized the opportunity of a pause to look at the group with what she hoped was a humble expression and speak to Fortune. 'Henry, when Jason arrived you were just about to tell me about the art in our bathroom.'

Perhaps forgetting that his dignity was undermined by his lime green shell-suit, Fortune turned towards her and put the tips of his fingers together. 'Ah, me,' he said. 'The bathroom. Yes, what we have…or appear to have…are a Piero Manzoni, a Terence Koh, and Wim Delvoye's sketch of "Cloaca." Magnificent! And how witty to locate them there!'

'Would you be kind enough to dilate a little on them for me?'

He looked at her pityingly and sighed. 'Where to start?'

'At the beginning. We have plenty of time.'

Fortune picked up his glass, sat back and looked at her over his glasses. 'It is hard to overestimate the influence of Piero Manzoni. Inspired by Lucio Fontana—of whose work our friend Charlie here recently has been lucky enough to secure a fine example—his ironic questioning of the nature of the art object would pre-figure conceptual art and become an inspiration for the *Arte Povera* movement.' He took a sip of champagne. 'I'll explain about that later.'

'How kind,' said the baroness, and reached for the bottle of claret resting on Joleen.

'Manzoni's father was a philistine.' The baroness repressed the desire to say 'like me,' and instead put on the fake interested look she had had to acquire many years before for professional purposes. 'He made tin cans. When he told Piero that he thought his art was shit, Piero conceived a magnificent response with an exhibition of ninety signed cans called *Merda d'artista*, priced by weight based on the then value of gold. Since then, of course, their intrinsic value has soared. Nick Serota got hold of one for the Tate for only £23,000 in 2000. He'd have had to pay more than £100,000 only a few years later.'

'Oh, my God,' said Marilyn. 'But that's less than forty thousand dollars. Chester, I've paid much much more for my three tins.'

'Yes, hon, but you didn't buy them until a few years later.'

'You bought three tins of shit?' asked Anastasia.

'Sure I did. But two of them were for museums.'

'What a generous woman you are,' said the baroness. 'You were saying, Henry. About Manzoni and…what do you call it?…*Arte Povera?*'

The condescension in his voice went up a notch. 'Piero's tragic death in 1963 at only twenty-nine predated a time of economic crisis when in Italy gifted radical young artists rejected the straitjacket of traditional expensive materials like bronze or canvas in favour of openness to, if you like, impoverished alternatives like wood and coal.' The baroness noted that Fortune seemed to be revelling in the sonorousness of his own voice. 'Another seminal moment in the development of conceptual art.' He sighed. 'I look at the Kounellis room in Tate Modern, and again, I envy Nick.'

'Thank you,' said the baroness, noting he seemed to have gone into a jealous reverie. 'And Koh?'

Fortune put his glass down on Joleen, shut his eyes and clasped his hands together. 'What a moment it was! Art Basel

2006! I'm embarrassed to say I had never heard of Terence Koh and then…aaah!…I was led to his installation.'

The baroness raised an enquiring eyebrow.

'It sounds so simple. Just eighty-eight glass cases, some of which had gold-plated pieces of what he said was his own excrement.'

'Why eighty-eight?'

'A lucky number in Chinese culture: the young man is Chinese-Canadian. So, as you can imagine, I thought of Manzoni; I thought of *Arta Povera*; I embraced the irony that is the combination of the poorest and the richest of materials. Collectors fought to buy the installation. Charles Saatchi lost out, but he gave Terence pride of place at his Royal Academy Show the next year.'

'We were late to Basel,' said Marilyn. 'Otherwise, I'd have got it.' Herblock patted her hand. 'You got so much else there, sweetie.'

'Nick has one in the series,' said Pringle. '*A New World Order Lies in this Golden Age*, but apparently what looks like excrement is entirely made of bronze.'

'Does that make it worth more or less?' asked Charlie Briggs, who seemed to be finding Fortune's lecture hard to follow.

'A good question, Charlie, but hard to answer. The market can be fickle.'

'What I find touching,' interjected Gavin Truss, 'is that Koh has made many hundreds of thousands of dollars from selling gold-plated shit—from what we call his conceptual bling period—but that he also cares about students, to whom he sells it in its natural state for only $150. As he points out, they're losing nothing, since his shit is worth its weight in gold.'

'Heart-warming,' said the baroness. 'And the sketch?'

'Wim Delvoye's sketch of his *Cloaca*,' said Fortune. 'The digestive machine he designed that turns food into faeces.'

'And its point is?' asked the baroness.

He shook his head at her stupidity. 'Its point is the pointlessness of life, since there is nothing more pointless than an elaborate machine that reduces food to waste. Mind you, I wonder if by selling the output he undermines his existential point.' He sighed. 'Ah, me! These are the unanswerable questions.'

The baroness replaced her glass on Joleen. 'May I make a few observations, Sir Henry?'

He gave a rather superior smirk. 'If you have any worth making.'

'Well, here are a few. Firstly, like Duchamp with his urinal, Manzoni was making a joke, not creating art. It was tough on him that he didn't stay alive long enough to savour it. I'm sure he deliberately spread the rumour that he might have cheated and that the contents might be other than promised, that is, not what it says on the tin.' The baroness never worried that obvious jokes had probably been made thousands of times before, so she snorted at her own wit. She was pleased to see that Fortune was looking furious.

'Manzoni would have loved the very conceptual-art dilemma that a can cannot be opened to see what is inside because if it's opened, the can will apparently no longer be a work of art. In the same way—as I learned from a recent visit to Tat Modern— Jeff Koons' hoovers will cease to be art if anyone turns one on.

'This is, of course, all bollocks. Tins of shit aren't art. Nor are hoovers and anyone who says they are is either soft in the head, corrupt, or a victim of mass hysteria.'

Fortune was sitting up and expostulating. She gestured at him to be quiet. 'Secondly, Terence Koh discovered, like many artists who preceded him, that the art world is dominated by people who care only for money, and that it can be taken from them in bucket-loads if you press the right buttons. Gold-plated shit isn't art: it's a novelty. The only people who could genuinely like it would be coprophiliacs. Like James Joyce.

'Thirdly, *Arte Povera* should be translated as poor art, except it isn't good enough to be poor. Mostly it isn't art at all. What is art in that ridiculous room in Tat Modern dedicated to the wretched Kounellis, the patriarch of that silly movement?'

'Silly? Silly? Oh, my God,' screamed Truss. 'You're talking about the D'Offay bequest that includes Kounellis' magnificent 1969 *Untitled*.'

'The bugger's too lazy to give any of his stuff a title. Are you talking about the sacks of lentils and various other dry goods? How are they art?'

'I bought a few of his Untitleds,' said Marilyn. 'Weren't they scribbles on a piece of paper, Chester?'

'I'm not sure which ones you got, sweetie, but I'm sure they were fine.'

'They'd better be. They cost more than a hundred K.'

'You've been very quiet,' said the baroness to Jake Thorogood. 'How are they art?'

He shrugged. 'Can't say I'm a great fan, but whatever floats your boat.'

'How can you say that?' said Hortense. 'I'm sure you've praised him in the past.'

'Very likely, Hortense. I write for a liberal newspaper, so I have to be right-on. But just at the moment, I'm not in the mood.'

The baroness looked at him with interest. 'You cared about great art once, Jake. I used to read you until you embraced the ugly and talentless. You really lost any scruples you ever had, didn't you?'

He shrugged again. Complete silence descended on the group. The baroness was contemplating how to get them arguing again when the disembodied voice broke in. 'Laidee Troutbeck to Diary Room.'

She threw herself into the chair and gazed at the camera. 'Was the argument what you wanted?'

'Good argument. You make them angry.'

'I certainly achieved that.'

'Who worst?'

'In what way worst?'

'You think worst.'

'Heavens, that's a big question with such a crew. I'd have to think.'

'I want answer now. Who worst this night?'

'An embarrassment of riches, but if you force me, Jake Thorogood annoyed me most. He knows better and he's not even hiding his corruption from himself.'

'Bedroom black door. Key on table. Say them choose bed. Now. Lights go after fifteen minutes.'

The baroness left him, walked past the group and unlocked the bedroom. Having surveyed it briefly, she turned round. 'We have a bedroom that should be to the liking of anyone who admires Tracey Emin, but I can't say I'm keen.'

The bedroom contained five double beds that looked as if they hadn't been made for weeks. They were all strewn with the same detritus that had made Emin famous. Neon lights around the room said: *'YOU HAD IT COMING', 'WHO'S SORRY NOW?', 'HERE TODAY, GONE TOMORROW'.* When she spotted the one saying *'JUST DESERTS,'* the baroness winced.

The housemates surveyed the stained sheets, the bottles, the used condoms and the rest. 'I'm not sleeping in that filth,' cried Marilyn.

'Nor me,' said Hortense. 'We can take sofas.'

The baroness signed. 'I'm sorry to have to tell you that Big Brother says if anyone doesn't sleep in a bed, there'll be no food tomorrow. I'm afraid Miss Emin has designed our beds and we must lie in them.'

Herblock took Marilyn's hand. 'Will you share one with me, hon?'

Henry Fortune was heard to say sotto voce to Pringle that no doubt he'd want to shack up with Charlie Briggs, but the response of 'Bubbles, how could you think that?' seemed sincere.

'Why don't you girls bunk in together?' asked Fortune of the baroness and Hortense, but the look of horror on both their faces put paid to that.

'I'll go with Gavin,' said Hortense.

'And then there were two,' said the baroness brightly. 'So it's me and Jake and Charlie and Anastasia. Or not.'

'It might be good for Charlie and Anastasia,' said Thorogood, 'but I fear nothing would induce me to share a bed with you.'

'I feel rather the same way.'

'Come on, Jack,' said Anastasia. 'We're mates now. I'm going to stick to you like shit to a blanket.'

'An unfortunate image when you think what we'll be sleeping on, Anastasia.'

Anastasia laughed merrily. 'Just call it art, Jack. Now let's go for it.'

In her violet shell-suit, the baroness tumbled into her disgusting bed feeling that indeed it was true that even the darkest cloud had a vestige of a silver lining. Not everyone felt that, for in a room containing ten people, five proved to be snorers. Still, they had all had so much to drink, that even the normally light sleepers eventually found oblivion and were so deeply asleep that they failed to notice four men coming softly into the bedroom and removing a comatose Jake Thorogood.

Pooley was shaving when the seven o'clock news told him a body had been found in the early hours hanging in the undercroft on the South Bank, and that foul play was suspected. Within five minutes he had dressed, kissed his sleeping wife, and was out of the door. He couldn't raise anyone at the Yard who seemed to know any more about the corpse, but he had a bad feeling.

By eight Pooley and Milton had informally identified Jake Thorogood's corpse from photographs. The official identification had to await his brother's arrival, but they were in no doubt. He'd been well dead when found at twenty past two in the morning. The pathologist was certain he'd been killed before midnight. 'Garrotted first with wire: hanged later with rope. As you can see, he was bollock naked and had a bunch of black balloons in his hand. Odd business. He'd had a lot to drink, but that hardly explains it.'

With the help of Morrison, palpably indignant at having to be back on duty so early, and of Sarah Byrne, who looked both upset and excited, the story was put together. 'I thought he was wearing an overcoat,' she said, 'but it fell off immediately. Like a loose shroud. Vernon cut the rope he was hanging from and we got him down, but he was cold and dead.'

'Go back to how you found him,' said Milton. 'And don't forget the placard.'

'Yes, well first I thought he was some kind of graffiti,' said Morrison. 'And when the wino said…'

'What wino?'

'The wino that told us he was there.'

'Where is he?'

'Dunno,' said Morrison.

'He disappeared while we were trying to resuscitate the deceased, sir,' said Byrne. 'Maybe he was scared. But I know what he looked like.'

'OK, Sarah. Go on, Vernon.'

'When the wino said there was a body in the corner in the middle of all that graffiti, I thought it was one of Banksy's vandalisms. I'd seen some of his stuff with hangin' men and balloons.' He paused. 'I tell a lie. The balloons were lifting some little girl, weren't they? But they were Banksy anyway. I think the wife bought a postcard of it once.

'Anyway, when we got to the corner, before the shroud fell off, I could see the word Banksy.'

'As you can see from these photos,' said Milton, 'it was attached to the garment.'

Morrison's brow furrowed. 'I didn't see that bit before Banksy,' he said. 'What's it say? Homidge? It's spelled wrong.'

'It's "o-maj,"' said Pooley. 'French. That's why it's spelled "*Hommage* to Banksy." And, underneath, "Man with Balloons," which is a reference to Banksy's *Girl with Balloons*.'

'That's a bit sick, isn't it, sir?'

'It certainly is, Sarah.'

'So what's with the 'ommidge word?'

'*Hommage* is close to the same meaning as our homage, Vernon, but where that means paying respect, according to the dictionary, o-maj means something expressive done in honour of someone using elements of their style.'

Morrison looked glazed.

'The murderer is paying *hommage* to Banksy in the manner in which he's killed Thorogood. Or,' added Pooley, who liked to be precise, 'has had him killed.'

Milton's phone rang. 'Thorogood's brother is here, Ellis. Look after him. I'll see you after I've seen the AC.'

He turned to the constables. 'Well done,' he said. 'Well observed and well handled. Congratulations.'

Morrison looked at him, hopeful they might be given extra time off in lieu. 'I know from experience,' said Milton, 'that when you've had a shock like this, the important thing is to go on as if nothing's happened. Go home and get some sleep now. I wish you a peaceful patrol tonight.'

◇◇◇

The nine were woken abruptly by the sound of a reveille and the voice saying 'Geddup you now.' In the ensuing *melée*, with shell-suited people flowing between bedroom and living room and bathroom and kitchen, no one realised for an hour that they were one short. The sheer joy of having showers and baths (free of the clothes that had been removed as they slept) distracted them pleasantly as much as the presence in the kitchen of basic breakfast ingredients.

There was a general attempt at civility so effective that the baroness even insisted on giving Fortune and Pringle the first pieces of toast she had extracted from the toaster. So it was not until breakfast was finished and they went into the living room that Charlie Briggs looked around and asked, 'Where's Jake?'

A quick search confirmed there was no Jake in any of the public rooms: the Diary Room was locked.

'He can't be gone,' screamed Pringle.

'He must have escaped,' said Briggs.

'How?' asked Anastasia. 'I've examined this shit hole from floor to ceiling and the only way out is that door over there that's locked and barred. It would take a battering ram to get it open.'

At that moment the voice instructed Laidee Troutbeck to go to the Diary Room, which proved now to be unlocked.

She threw herself into the vast chair. On the table before her was a pile of pads and pencils. 'Where's Jake Thorogood?'

'He is place of dead person.'

'You mean the morgue?'

'Yes.'

'Are you serious, Ol…Big Brother?'

'Oh, yes. I serious man.'

'Why would you want to kill him?'

'He cheat me. He say Banksy real Banksy but not real Banksy.' Sarkovsky sniggered. 'So my men killing him. With balloons. Your idea.'

'My idea?'

'You say you killing Banksy with balloons.'

The baroness' head was spinning. 'Did Thorogood cost you a fortune with the fake Banksy?'

'Not beeg money. Small money, but he make Oleg appeeer stupid man.'

'And that's enough reason to murder him?'

'Nobody make Oleg Sarkovsky appeeer stupid man. I execute.'

'I don't know if I believe you, but if I tell them what you've said there will be mass hysteria and there'll be no arguments.'

'You say them anything. I not interest.'

'So if I say he's just been evicted, you won't contradict me?'

'What means this contradeect?'

'Say I am wrong.'

'Maybe. Maybe not.'

'Presumably you're angry with everyone. Why did you choose him?'

'You say worst.'

She began to expostulate and then stopped. What was the point of arguing with a lunatic? Damage limitation was the order of the day. And dragging things out in the hope that the cavalry would ride over the range before it was too late.

'May I go back to them?'

'Give them paper and pencil and say them drawing.'

'Draw what?'

'Horse. Horse eating. Horse running. Horse fucking. Then lunch and drink. Then argument again. Then game.'

'Game?'

'I say later.'

The baroness got up and began to collect the materials. 'Laidee Troutbeck.'

'Yes, Big Brother.'

'You say me this night who worst.'

'I've never even seen a dead body,' said Max Thorogood. 'It's a shock. Especially when you're not expecting it and it's your kid brother.'

Pooley muttered consolatory phrases. 'May I get you coffee, Mr. Thorogood?'

'Yes, please. Are we going to talk about Jake?'

'If you're up to it.'

When they had both been furnished with indifferent liquid, Thorogood had a sip and grimaced. 'So what's happened?'

'We don't really know any more than is in the newspapers, Mr. Thorogood, though we do have a line of enquiry that we can't yet discuss.'

'No surprises there.'

'Is there anything you think might help us?'

'Don't think so, Chief Inspector. I haven't really known Jake since we were kids. There were just the two of us and we fought the way boys do, wrestling around the garden, fighting for the honour of our football teams. All that kind of thing. But I looked out for him when we were at school and protected him from the kids who thought he had airs and graces. But we were chalk and cheese. I went off to train as an actuary and I know he despised me for doing something so dull. Then he said he wanted to do a fine arts degree and at first I tried to take an interest. Mum and Dad used to take us to art galleries a bit and I knew my Rembrandt from my Reubens.

'For a while, I loved listening to Jake talking about artists and I was so proud when he became an art critic. I'd read his review every week. We didn't really see each other. No fallings out. But how could you expect us to have anything in common any more? Mum and Dad died early, I was living in Salford with a wife who was a district nurse and two children. Jake was being paid to go to glamorous places with glamorous people and he didn't want to commit, so there was a succession of gorgeous girls of the kind who hang about that world wanting to be famous or rich.

'But then what he wrote stopped seeming real. He seemed to be obsessed with fashionable. I hate to say it, with my little bro lying dead in that morgue and me terrified that he might have had a really horrible death, but he sold out along the way. I don't know if it was to fashion or to money, but as an actuary, I'd say it might be a bit of both. It takes courage for a critic to hold out against the herd and, if you're hanging out with the mega-rich, it would be really heroic not to want a bit of the action. I mean, you're going to say the Tate Modern is full of rubbish and expect to get good commissions? Pul-ease!'

He had another sip of his coffee, made a face and put it on the table. 'Did he die because he sold out, Chief Inspector?'

Pooley had found a minute to send a text to Amiss and Mary Lou telling them the news, so Amiss was primed and ready for Milton's press conference. He briefly expressed regret at having to announce that Thorogood had been murdered, told them where the body had been found, refused to give any further information for the moment, admitted there were concerns for the well-being of the other nine hostages, assured them the police were working flat-out to find them, denied having any idea who was responsible, and then excused himself and went back into the Yard.

Pausing only to text Rachel, Amiss rang Miss Stamp.

'Oh, Mr. Amiss, I'm so glad to hear from you. Is there any news? We're frantic here. And those dreadful journalists keep snooping around asking questions about the mistress. We won't let them in but we can't keep them out of the grounds. They been hammering on the door and peering through the windows all morning. And I've had to put the phone down on several of them already.'

'I'm afraid there is worrying news, Miss Stamp. Jake Thorogood, one of those who went missing at the same time as the mistress, has been found murdered. It's just been announced.'

There was a terrified squawk. 'Oh, Mr. Amiss, that's terrible. What happened to him? Is there no possibility it was an accident?'

'I'm afraid he was strangled and then hanged. The police are sure it was murder.'

'The mistress must be in terrible danger. Why haven't the police found her?'

'I don't know, Miss Stamp. We must remember what an optimist she is and think like her. And we know she's indestructible.'

He heard a sob and felt like joining in. 'Let us do what we can to help her. I need to get hold of the mistress' friend Myles Cavendish who's abroad and won't know anything about this. Do you have his mobile number?'

'I wouldn't have that, Mr. Amiss. You know how secretive the mistress is about her private life.'

'I do, Miss Stamp. Can you go through any address books she has and maybe old diaries?'

'Oh, Mr. Amiss. Won't she be annoyed?'

'I think I can safely say that if she could, Miss Stamp, she would give you *carte blanche.*'

'I'll run up and search her study now, Mr. Amiss. But it could take quite a while.'

'And if there's nothing written down, Miss Stamp, you might need to explore her computer. She does have one, doesn't she?'

'Yes and no, Mr. Amiss. She hates it, but she learned to do email. First I'll look for diaries.'

'Is there news of Jake?' asked Pringle.

'I'm told he had a stomach upset during the night and had to be taken to a doctor. It looks like he's got a nasty infection, so he may not be back.'

'Why are you always the go-between with Big Brother,' asked Fortune. 'It seems very suspicious to me.'

'And me,' said Pringle. Most of the others nodded.

'After all, how do we know you're passing on the instructions correctly? And are you an experienced negotiator?'

'I don't know,' said the baroness. 'I wouldn't have chosen the role. Maybe he wants me because I'm the oldest. Anyway, since he's listening in much of the time, presumably he thinks I'm reporting to him correctly. Now get cracking,' she said. 'He would like us to draw horses doing anything horses do.'

'Why?' asked Briggs. 'I can't draw.'

'I can't draw either, Charlie, but we are guests of Big Brother and if he wants us to draw, I suggest we should do our best. If we do, I've been promised that we'll have lunch to follow, accompanied by wine. If we don't, there won't be any lunch.' She didn't mention she had had a great deal of difficulty in persuading Sarkovsky to use the carrot of lunch rather than the stick of murder.

The inmates set to with a will. The baroness, who hadn't sketched since school, found to her surprise that she produced something that closely resembled a horse, even if its legs seemed worryingly splayed. After an hour, she surveyed the results. Apart from Marilyn—who admitted to having once had a home art tutor and was competent —the older generation achieved mediocrity. Having been taught to draw at school, they managed to draw animals that were identifiably equine. Briggs was bad and Anastasia was hopeless: no one not on hallucinatory drugs could have seen a horse anywhere in her bold and talentless lines.

The baroness was intensely relieved that there would be a pause for food, drink, and argument before she had to go back to the Diary Room to make a judgement. The gathering had passed that stage of hunger when they would have fallen on gruel with shrieks of gratitude, but they were still rather pathetically grateful for having a choice of several pizzas as well as a decent claret.

Although the baroness' philosophy of life was so *carpe diem* that she always saw the glass as half-full, her appetite was severely blunted by the knowledge of what she would have to do that evening. Besides which, she didn't think much of the pizza.

Chapter Nine

Amiss had spent the rest of the morning at his computer, continuing his obsessive hunt for news, which was broken only by worried conversations with friends. It was just after midday when George, the homeless man who had led the police to the body, turned up at the offices of a national newspaper and offered his story in exchange for help in getting off the streets. And so it was that by early afternoon Milton had to come clean about the balloons and the placard. The '*Hommage* Murder' went viral on the Internet.

A certain calm had descended on the group after lunch, which the baroness realised she had to dispel. She poured out some more wine into all the glasses on offer. She was sparing with hers, for she had concluded if you have the power of life and death, you shouldn't use it when half-cut. 'Just from curiosity,' she asked, 'what do we think of each other's horses? Gavin, perhaps you'd care to tell us why we have in this dungeon a cross-section of those who dominate art, and between us only one of us is better than pathetic.'

'There's photography these days. Why should anyone need to draw a horse?' asked Truss.

Charlie Briggs' brown furrowed. 'You mean that art has nothing to add to a photo?'

'Not a lot,' said Truss. 'Since the camera, there's no point.'

'If photos can replace art,' asked the baroness, 'why is Stubbs' *Whistlejacket* the main draw in the National Gallery?'

'Because tourists know no better,' said Hortense Wilde.

'Stubbs spent a great deal of his life dissecting horses so as to understand how muscle and bone and spirit interacted,' said the baroness. 'He gave us many portraits that have enchanted generations and in *Whistlejacket*, he showed us the majesty of the horse and the brilliance of the humble artist. What do you offer instead?'

'We must move on,' said Hortense. 'That's why dreary old-fashioned skills are so unimportant. They might momentarily matter to a generation stuck in the past, but today's technology replaces them.'

'Like what,' asked the baroness politely.

'A drawing app.'

'If I'm not mistaken, Hortense, David Hockney, possibly our best artist of the last fifty years, uses technology as a tool of his art but deplores the fact that the young are no longer imparted any skills.'

Hortense laughed mirthlessly. 'Oh, for heaven's sake, Jack. Hockney! Really! For God's sake, he does landscapes. Since the world was changed by Damien, how is Hockney even shown?'

'So you didn't like his Royal Academy show? I thought it fine and so did tens of thousands of others.'

Hortense looked at her with an expression so patronising it was as much as the baroness could do not to hit her. Then she remembered what she might have to do to her, and the impulse passed.

'Who cares what the public think?' asked Hortense. 'What do they know? Their opinion is worth nothing.'

'Tell me something, Hortense. If this minute you could replace all this Hirst stuff with Stubbs by waving a wand, what would you do?'

Hortense looked around her, caught sight of the cow's head and shuddered.

'Oh, for God's sake, be honest,' said Briggs. 'This whole fucking place is a nightmare. Smelly dead cows and flies and murder weapons. Anything would be better.'

'Yeah,' said Anastasia. 'I'd like something cheerful.'

Fortune assumed his most pompous voice. 'At least we have great art here, Anastasia. Are you suggesting we'd be better off with Jack Vitriano or Beryl Cook?'

Pringle and Truss laughed sycophantically.

'I've seen some Beryl Cook,' said Anastasia. 'All those cheerful fat women having a ball. Yes, I'd trade them in for all the ghoulish stuff any day.'

'And I like Vitriano,' said Briggs. 'Do you remember, Jason? I wanted to buy one of his but you said everyone would laugh at me.'

'And I was right, Charlie. No decent critic or curator would touch either of those pathetic bourgeois throwbacks. The hedge-fundies know that.'

'If I ever get out of here,' said Briggs, 'I will never take anyone's advice about art again.'

A silence descended. Then the dreaded voice sounded. 'Now you play game. Laidee Troutbeck, Diary Room.'

'So, what did the AC say, Jim?' asked Pooley.

'He's finally got it and he's alarmed. Just for now he's OK'd the surveillance, but he hasn't decided yet if we should look for a warrant. He's having another think.'

'And the commissioner?'

'The AC said he'll be back tomorrow and expressly forbade me from bothering him in the middle of his important discussions at the Interpol conference.' Milton shrugged. 'What can I do?

'Doesn't he get it?'

'Doesn't he get what?'

'Thorogood is just the first.'

'How can you know that?'

'There are ten of them. As far as we know, the worst Thorogood did to Sarkovsky was to give him a bum steer on something which by his standards cost small change. Allegra thought it was less than a million. Thorogood was a critic, for God's sake, Jim. Not an international swindler of oligarchs.'

'Did his brother know anything helpful?'

'He thought he'd sold out, which is what Jack said. But Sarkovsky is a scoundrel, so why should he get prissy about Thorogood lacking ethics?'

'Because his lack of ethics cost Sarkovsky money, I suppose. '

'In cahoots with Pringle and Fortune. Anyway, what we have to face is that if Thorogood, whose sins were minor, ended up the way he has, why should anyone else be safe?'

'I get that.'

'Worse.'

'There's worse?'

'You know that evening with Jack in ffeatherstonehaugh's that you missed.'

'Well, seeing I missed it, not really.'

'I told you a bit about it. The endless diatribe against contemporary art.'

'So?'

'I didn't tell you about her fantasies.'

'Gimme a break, Ellis. What fantasies?'

'Her fantasies about how to kill conceptual artists in the manner of their art.'

'As in "*Hommage* to Banksy."'

'I'm afraid so.'

'Would you mind getting us some more coffee, Ellis? I need my wits about me.'

'So Jim's worried that when he tells this to the AC, he'll go back to assuming Jack's a serial murderer.'

'But for heaven's sake, Ellis,' said Amiss, 'can't he explain to the cretin that she'll have been describing those fantasies far and wide and she'll certainly have told them to Sarkovsky. To amuse him.'

'He didn't have much of a sense of humour, did he?'

'No. She said custard pies in the face, cripples falling off their zimmers, and generally other people's misfortunes were the kind of thing that made him laugh.'

'That's ominous.'

'It sure is.'

'My mind's working overtime, Ellis. Is yours?'

'If he's killed one, he means to kill them all.'

'I'm afraid so.'

'Maybe he's done it already.'

'He's more likely to be stringing it out.'

'He's got to be in London, hasn't he?'

'Looks like it. We've got people checking out his apartment building now and trying to find out if he's been sighted. And we're digging up what info we can.'

'Time isn't on your side.'

'You're telling me.'

'I'm going to try to track down Myles. If you bastards can't find her, it's time to bring in the SAS.'

'I didn't hear that,' said Pooley.

'Sorry. Of course you didn't, since I never said it. What I said was that Jack's close friend Myles needs to know she's disappeared. Is there a number for him among whatever material you took out of their flat?'

'Don't think so. It's very much a *pied-à-terre*. No papers to speak of. Mary Lou might have some idea.'

Miss Stamp was trying to keep calm. 'I've searched high and low but I can't find the mistress' address book, Mr. Amiss. She must have had it with her. And I can't get into her computer because I don't know her password. I've tried variations on Troutbeck and St. Martha's, but no luck. But then I wouldn't know what numbers to add. I tried the year of her birth, but that didn't work either.'

'If I had to guess I'd think of British military triumphs, Miss Stamp. Try Waterloo1815 or Trafalgar1805.'

She giggled rather forlornly. 'That would be like her, Mr. Amiss. I'll try them and telephone you back.'

It took five minutes before a disconsolate Miss Stamp reported in the negative. However Amiss' next suggestion,

'Agincourt1415,' did the trick. It took only a couple of minutes for her to find Myles Cavendish's email address and phone number. Amiss sent an email as well as text and voice messages into the blue and went out to pace around the park, leaving Plutarch draped over his computer, shedding hair all over his keyboard and desk.

The baroness had never watched Big Brother and no one but Anastasia and Charlie Briggs admitted having seen it, but they had told stories that gave everyone a flavour of what was to be expected from a game. By now they were all ready to hear they might be required to dress up in skin-tight lurex cat-suits and perform ungraceful dances, or dress as pastry chefs and throw pies at each other. However the news that this game was to be conducted in the nude caused a minor sensation.

'I won't do it,' shouted Henry Fortune. 'I will not sacrifice my dignity.'

'Me neither,' said Hortense.

'You play game,' said the voice of Big Brother. 'Or evicted. If evicted, die.'

'He can't really mean that,' wailed Pringle. 'Can he? Is that what happened to Jake?'

Eight heads turned towards the baroness.

'You said he'd been taken ill,' said Pringle.

She thought of trying to keep the fiction going, but realised Sarkovsky's intervention had made it pointless. 'He was evicted. And no, I don't know if that means he's been killed, but I doubt it. However, just in case, I guess it makes sense to do what Big Brother wants.'

'That way we lose our dignity and then we die anyway,' said Fortune.

'Perhaps,' said the baroness. 'But perhaps not. Big Brother may well be joking. Best to keep the options open, I'd say.'

'Oh, Bubbles, you must, you must, you must. It's not as if we're on television. No one will see us.'

There was what sounded like a low snigger.

'Oh, God,' cried Fortune. 'Maybe we are.'

'For heaven's sake, Henry,' said the baroness, 'if we were on television it would be good news. It would make us easier to find. Now if I were you, I'd focus on survival and do what we've been asked to do.

'In the hatch, I'm told, are canvasses and pots of paint. We get a canvas each and we are to paint it using our naked body as the only means of transferring paint to surface. Shall we fetch the materials now and lay them out? Then we can disrobe.'

The baroness regretted that the knot of dread that would not unravel had stifled her sense of humour, for, at other times, she would have been mightily amused by what went on that afternoon. It was Hortense who had said maybe the thing was to attempt to emulate Jackson Pollock and his drip paintings and with Fortune and Truss produced dollops of pretentious guff on the subject, with a bit of a disagreement about whether he was a genius because of the fractal dimensions of his work or because of his role as a progressive purifier of form.

The baroness, who had been known to throw her newspaper at the wall when she read that yet another Pollock jumble had gone for nine figures, had pointed out rather coldly that they had to go a stage further than the maestro since Big Brother insisted that they couldn't pour paint on the canvas but actually had to apply it with bits of their body. What's more, he had forbidden them to use their digits to apply paint to canvas. Hands were out, and so were toes, though they could be used to put paint on their bodies. And what was even more challenging, no two people were to use the same bit of their body and no one could help anyone else. This information induced a kind of terrified paralysis among several of the gathering.

'We'll have to negotiate who uses what,' said the baroness. 'First come, first served, I think.'

'If I wanted to make a mint out of this in my past life,' observed Anastasia, 'I'd have stuck paint up my fanny and let it drip out.'

'I don't want to act as the health and safety officer, Anastasia, but I'd confine paint to the outside rather than the inside if I were you. Any other suggestions?'

'Isn't there some Russian Sheila who paints with her breasts? I once thought about trying that.'

'Now's your chance,' said the baroness, 'unless Marilyn or Hortense want to counter bid?'

They shook their heads. 'Elbow,' said Marilyn. 'Knee,' said Herblock. 'Shoulder blades,' said Hortense. 'Head,' said Truss.

'Didn't that Riverdance bloke put paint on the soles of his shoes and tap dance on a canvas?' asked Briggs.

'You won't be wearing shoes, Charlie, but there's no reason not to try that if no one objects.'

No one did. 'Bum,' said the baroness. 'As in, I'll paint with it. Now that leaves just Henry and Jason. I'm afraid there aren't many options left for you.'

'I was too shocked to think,' said Fortune. 'What's left?'

'Your stomach?'

'How can I paint with my stomach, you madwoman?'

'Just slap a few colours on and move the canvass around it.'

'Oh, all right. I suppose I could do that.'

'What about me?' screamed Pringle. 'Am I supposed to use my willie?'

There was a silence until the baroness said, 'Unless you can think of anything else.'

'I can't,' sobbed Pringle.

Anastasia patted him on the back. 'You won't be the first to do it, Jason. There's a drongo back home calls himself "Pricasso." He makes a living out of it and it doesn't seem to do him any harm.'

The baroness stood up and clapped her hands. 'Excellent. That's all settled. Now, shall we make a start? It might be less daunting if we all do it together.'

Apart from Anastasia and Briggs, they were as unappetising a collection as might have been found in any naturist encampment for seniors. At one extreme were the scrawny, like Pringle and Marilyn, and at the other the portly, like Fortune and the baroness. By unspoken agreement, they tried to avoid looking at each other.

Anastasia went to work with a will. After trial and error, her favoured approach was to dip each breast in paint of a different colour and press the canvas against first one, then the other, and then rub it with both. Since he found it difficult to keep within the constraints of the canvas, Briggs seems more like a dancer on hot-coals than another Michael Flatley, but he became quite interested in the process and kept going back for more paint to smear on his feet.

Marilyn's sharp elbow proved to be a precision instrument. She chose black paint exclusively and aimed for geometric patterns. Herblock's knee was less successful, not least because at the beginning he tried to do it standing on one leg and fell over twice. Hortense obviously hadn't thought her choice through properly. It caused her acute discomfort actually to get enough paint from hand to shoulder blade, and it proved even more difficult to find a way of transferring it to the canvas.

Being shaven, Truss' choice of head had been sensible, though sometimes he miscalculated the density of the paint and ended up with much of it running down his face before he could bend over to apply it to the canvas. The baroness approached her task stoically, smearing different colours onto her buttocks and then rubbing the canvas up down and across them. Watching her technique gave Fortune courage and inspiration, and he completed his picture quickly, which gave him the time and psychic space to urge Pringle on. 'No, Jay. Not the tip. Just smear it along the sides and rub it in sideways. That's it. You've got it. You've got it. That's the way.'

'You can't talk to Ellis about this, Mary Lou.'

'I know I can't. He'd have to turn us in if he knew we were looking to getting a private army on to this. Yet I don't think legal methods are likely to work, do you?'

'Can't say I'm very hopeful, especially at the pace at which they're going. They've only just got started on looking for a property that Sarkovsky might own through a company. And apparently there was a long discussion about whether the wheels should be set in motion to ask the security services to track Sarkovsky's phone. Anyway, there's no harm in talking to Myles about it. He'll make his own decisions.'

'Do you by any chance have an alternative number for Myles? I've heard nothing back.'

'Nope. I barely know him.'

'It's ridiculous, isn't it? They've been an item—well, a sort of an item—for years, but we almost never see him.'

'I think they both like it that way. It's a relationship that allows them to do whatever the hell they like and I fancy he's as secretive and compartmentalised as she is.'

'I just hope he's as resourceful.'

'Me too,' said Mary Lou. 'This sucks. This really really sucks.'

On his way home, Martin Conroy read yet another of those property articles about what the mega-rich went in for. He had seen several about the new fashion for digging deep under big houses to create an enormous basement for one's swimming pool, gym, and spa. Apparently now real opulence had become the name of the game, with Turkish baths, Italianate spas, movie theatres, and golf-simulation centres. He wondered if the house in north London that had been bought by the latest Sarkovsky company he had tracked down had been a likely candidate for such improvements. Certainly, enormous sums had been spent until the money suddenly dried up.

Conroy didn't yet know what overall was the state of Sarkovsky's finances, but things looked terrible. The bloke must be getting really desperate. He decided to see what builders he'd been using and if they were legit.

'Max Thorogood's been very helpful,' said Pooley to Milton, who was slumped, exhausted, at his desk. 'Turned out he was Jake's only heir, so what with the solicitor, the accountant, the bank, and his newspaper, I've already got an idea of what was going on with him financially. His salary was £80,000, but he had extra income over the past few years in the region of a quarter-of-a-million for consultancy services to Jason Pringle.'

'And consultancy means?'

'Shady authentication for Pringle, I suppose.'

'Well, he's certainly paid a heavy price. Sarkovsky, if it's him, is clearly not a forgiving man. And all the information I'm getting about him suggests that even as oligarchs go, he's a ruthless bastard.' He looked at his watch. 'It's ten o'clock, Ellis. We've been here for more than fourteen hours. God knows what horrors tomorrow will bring. Let's go home and get some sleep.'

Bizarrely, the shared ludicrous task had for the first time induced some sense of community spirit. Being naked and covered with paint was a great leveller. The baroness briefly revelled in the absence of hate. It was short-lived, for Sarkovsky had decreed that there must be another argument before bedtime. And before she was required to choose the worst.

When Hortense and Pringle, the stragglers, had finished, the baroness clapped her hands and said, 'Big Brother wants us to decide who has created art.'

'I have,' said Anastasia, displaying her smears. 'If I think it's art, it's art. Isn't that what we've been told to believe?'

'Is it true, Henry?'

'If she thinks it is, it is.'

'That's the kind of fatuous nonsense that has ruined our galleries and art schools,' said the baroness. 'If everything's art, nothing's art.'

Somehow, the mainly middle-aged or elderly paint-spattered people couldn't work up the enthusiasm to argue. Duty called the baroness. 'Is this art?' she asked, presenting her multi-coloured bottom to the audience.

'Don't be absurd,' said Hortense. 'Of course it isn't. You're not an artist.'

'If it was Anastasia's bottom—leaving the aesthetic out of it—would it be art?'

'It would have to be selected by a gallery,' said Pringle. 'There has to be a filter operated by people who know.'

'People like you?'

'Indeed.'

'Tell me, Jason, if the Mona Lisa was lying outside your gallery in the gutter, would it be art?'

'Of course. It has been validated and exhibited.'

'If that had never happened, it wouldn't be art?'

'This is puerile,' said Fortune.

'This is totalitarian,' said the baroness. 'You people have set yourselves up as arbiters of taste, and you made arbitrary decisions that suit you professionally. That is why Charlie—in his innocence—spent five million quid on something that when your world comes to its senses, will be a joke. For that amount of money he could have bought a Georgian country house, roomfuls of beautiful furniture, good silver, fine sculpture, and paintings his children would have been proud of.'

'Did we really sleep in art last night, Jason?' asked Briggs.

'Of course not, it was counterfeit Tracey, not original."

'Do we know that?' asked Briggs. 'Maybe Big Brother bought the original.'

'Nonsense,' said Hortense. 'It's not for sale.'

'But suppose it had been, and he'd bought it, and created four identical copies. Would the original have been art and all the others not?' enquired the baroness.

'Of course,' said Hortense.

'Yes,' said Fortune.

'Yes,' said Truss.

'Everyone agree?'

'Not me,' said Anastasia.

'Or me,' said Briggs. 'Now I think about it, it's all a ginormous con trick.'

'Like the Olafur Eliasson nonsense for the Olympics London Festival,' said the baroness.

Pringle produced another signature scream.

'You are unremittingly ignorant, aren't you?' said Fortune. 'The concept is thrilling.'

'Rubbish. The fellow's a fraud.'

Seven shocked faces looked at her, but Anastasia seemed amused. 'A fraud,'cried the baroness. 'A hundred carat fraud. He's been given a million quid to encourage people around the world to breathe. What bollocks!'

'Oh, dear, oh dear,' said Fortune. 'Clearly, you've missed the point of *Take a Deep Breath*.' He shook his head patronisingly. 'Such an astonishing, uplifting end to the Olympics. He will encourage global connectivity.'

'Global connectivity my arse. He will encourage global derision for British culture. Only we could be mad enough to hire a Danish charlatan to produce an invisible piece of art and call it a tribute to British culture.' She slammed her glass down on Trixie. 'It isn't even bloody original. Y'all being experts presumably remember our friend Piero Manzoni's *Artist's Breath*—those balloons filled with his own breath that he used to flog before he opted for the more lucrative shit.

'My God,' she said, warming to her theme, 'don't you realise this is a perfect example of emperor's new clothes? A piece of art that doesn't actually exist? An artistic equivalent of that wally John Cage's piece of silent music.'

Hortense Wilde's face darkened. 'If you wish to describe one of the musical geniuses of the twentieth century as a wally, I suppose I can't stop you. You merely show your ignorance. You are, I suppose, in your crass way, referring to his magnificent *4'33*.'

'His what?' asked Anastasia.

'The master's favourite work,' said Hortense reverentially. 'The high-point of his exploration of indeterminacy. A musical counterpoint to Rauschenberg's *White Paintings*.'

'Huh?'

'Rauschenberg was a modernist who exhibited blank canvasses that inspired Cage,' said the baroness. 'Cage's contribution to pretending nothing was something consisted of four minutes and thirty-three seconds when musicians sat there not playing.

'The silence was performed at various times by anything from a solitary pianist to a full symphony orchestra.'

'But that's crazy,' said Anastasia.

'Sounds funny to me,' said Charlie Briggs.

'You don't understand,' broke in Pringle. 'The sounds the audience make become the music. It varies from performance to performance. Genius. As Rauschenberg's white paintings could register lighting.'

'Sounds like this dickhead who's getting the world to breathe so he doesn't have to make anything,' said Anastasia.

'Anyone who doesn't appreciate Cage and Eliasson has no imagination,' said Hortense. 'In art the progressive is all.'

'You're just an old-fashioned cultural Marxist, Hortense, isn't that it?'

'"Why is progressive good?' asked Anastasia. 'Isn't good good and crap crap?'

'Anastasia,' asked Fortune, 'do you know what you are saying?'

'I'm saying that a lot of modern art is rubbish. And that includes what I do myself.'

'I'm going to ignore that,' said Fortune. 'It's patently untrue. If it were rubbish, Jason would not have exhibited and dealt in it, Jake would not have endorsed it, and I would not have purchased it for public view.'

'Oh, yes you would,' said the baroness and Anastasia together. Fortune ignored the baroness. 'You're upset, Anastasia. It's understandable. We're all under strain. Let's get back to the Olympics.'

'Yes, let's,' said the baroness. 'Leaving this Eliasson creature out of it, the art associated with it is an unmitigated disaster.'

'How can you say that?' asked Marilyn. 'That guy Kapoor's a genius. Don't you get the magnificence of *Orbit*.'

'Genius?' cried the baroness. 'Anish bloody Kapoor has provided the Olympic Park with a four hundred foot erection of red squiggles—a helter-skelter—that people can climb up. At a cost of more than twenty million quid! Admittedly, it's paid for by Indian steel billionaires, but we have to put up with the world thinking we think it's art.'

'How can you so fail to appreciate a magnificent monument to instability?' asked Hortense.

'Very very easily,' said the baroness, breathing heavily. 'Kapoor's become the high priest of fairground art. Look what he did mucking up rooms in the Royal Academy by shooting shells of red wax from a cannon. Oh, yes, and giving another over to distorting mirrors. He's a funfair sort of guy. That's why Nicholas Bloody Serota is such a fan.'

Pringle burst into tears. 'I don't care,' he said. 'I just want to be out of here.'

Exhausted, everyone fell silent.

'Laidee Troutbeck to Diary Room. Now.'

As the baroness trudged off, she wondered if she could cope. She was an optimist, so she didn't really believe that she would be sending someone to their death. But she was also a realist, who knew it was possible. And she also knew that while she was a woman of strong opinions and a deep sense of right and wrong, she was unhappy being what now appeared to be a hanging judge. She knew equally that the easy way out would be to refuse to choose. But she knew too that this would be a contemptible route. 'I never expected,' she said to herself, 'to be forced into making Sophie's Choice. But if that's what's going on, that's what I have to do. They may not be children, but I will try to protect the most innocent. And, of course, myself.'

Chapter Ten

It was two a.m, and Morrison and Sarah were on patrol.

'I felt bad about Sarah Byrne,' Milton had said to Pooley earlier that day, 'but I know what a lazy bastard Morrison is and I knew he'd want time off and I wasn't going to pander to him. Anyway, we're overstretched.'

Morrison was indeed aggrieved. 'He's got a nerve, expecting us to patrol by the Thames again,' said Morrison. 'Aren't we allowed any time to get over the shock of findin' a stiff?'

'I guess it's regarded as part of our job, Vernon.'

'I think we should get a special allowance for it.'

'Like a bonus?'

'Well, not like a bonus. More like compo. We sure need some extras now they're slashing overtime.'

As instructed, they walked all the way around Parliament Square, gingerly avoiding the remaining few protestors' tents. 'Effin' layabouts,' said Morrison. 'Honestly, some people have no work ethic.'

Byrne let that pass. They crossed the street and began to walk by the House of Commons. Morrison jerked his head in the direction of Oliver Cromwell's statue. 'Now there's a bloke who knew what to do with layabouts. Off with their heads. That'd sort them out. He'd have known what to do with all the wankers cheatin' on their expenses too.'

'It's nice when it's crisp like this,' said Byrne.

'Crisp? Bloody cold if you ask me. We shouldn't have to be out poundin' pavements in this weather. All that crap about takin' us out of cars so we could mingle with the public.' He waved crossly at the House of Commons. 'What effin' public? Everyone's gone home.'

'There may be more people on the other side of the river, Vernon.'

'I don't want more people,' he said mutinously. 'And I don't want to walk all the way to that bloody Tate Modern. No one will know if we don't.'

'It's our job to do it, Vernon. We should cross Westminster Bridge now.'

"I dunno what makes you such a glutton for punishment, Sarah. Why do you want to look for trouble?'

'The Sarge said…'

'I don't care what the Sarge said. It's OK for him, nice and snug back at HQ while he orders the likes of us to trudge the streets. Well, I don't know about you, but I'm not a slave.' He puffed up his chest. 'I'm not going any farther without a tea and a sausage sandwich. We'll go to the cabbie shelter at Embankment and I'll cross the river then.'

Not for the first time, Byrne fantasised about kicking Morrison right in the middle of his paunch. 'OK,' she said, 'but we'd better make it quick.'

No one's temper was improved by their being refused service at the cabbie shelter, but Morrison eventually got hold of a sausage in a fast-food joint in Villiers Street, and Byrne was able to steer him towards Waterloo Bridge. 'We've got to walk fast, Vernon, or they'll want to know what's been keeping us.' She accelerated. Knowing himself to be in the wrong, Morrison sulked. Wearily, for she was no more a fan of late-night walking than was he, she drew on the old reliable ploy. 'So did you decide which train to buy, Vernon? You were very conflicted when we talked about it last.'

The monologue went on and on and on, but it allowed Byrne to think about what she had to think about, which was mostly child care arrangements. The division of labour between her mother and mother-in-law was beginning to show fault lines. She wrestled with her choices, as Morrison wrestled with his, until Tate Modern hove in view.

'You ever been to this, Sarah?'

'No. Have you?'

'No.'

'But I've been to the other Tate. Tate Britain. I used to go there sometimes with my school. I really liked it. Specially the Turners.'

Morrison snorted. 'I've seen them too. Good stuff. But I'll never go again since I went to see the Turner Prize years back.'

'Because?'

'Because it was bloody crap, that's why. Just a bare room with a light goin' on and off. I think the artist even had the bare cheek to call it *Lights Goin' On and Off*. If you ask me, he was having a laugh. When I went home I wrote a letter sayin' that if that was the best they could do they didn't deserve any of my taxes. That modern art. A toddler could do it. And as for this Tate Modern? Did you know they're fillin' it with Damien Hirst's rubbish? The idea is that during the Olympics foreigners will be shown the best of British art. They've even had to reinforce the floors because of all them animals and fish he's had killed for his so-called art. It's not right. I mean I know I eat them, but that's different. It's natural.'

They left the street and walked towards the building. The area was deserted. Even the large grassy area in front of it seemed unoccupied. 'Too chilly there for winos,' said Morrison. 'OK, let's walk round it like the Sarge said and then we can get the hell out of it and go back to base.'

It was then they saw the large, rectangular object that seemed to be obstructing part of the entrance. 'What's that?' exploded Morrison. 'They're leavin' their stupid art outside now where anyone can smash it up. For God's sake, it's made of glass. Any bloody vandal could take a brick to it. No trouble. Not that it'd be any loss.'

Byrne found her torch and switched it on. 'Oh, God, Vernon. Look. It's a naked woman. Floating.'

They surveyed the object. 'It's one of them Damien Hirst things, isn't it,' asked Morrison. 'Didn't he do a dead shark in a tank like this? But this isn't a dead shark.'

'It isn't. It's a dead woman.'

'It'll be a mannequin, won't it?'

Byrne crouched beside the vitrine and shone her torch up and down. 'Don't think so, Vernon. Look. Her mouth's wide open. And you don't get mannequins with bunions.' She shone her torch around the side. 'Vernon! There's a card here.'

'What does it say?'

'*Hommage* to Hirst. And underneath—*The Physical Impossibility of Creating Art When You've No Fucking Talent.*'

'It's another one of 'em. Isn't it?'

''Fraid so,' said Byrne, her voice quavering. She ran to the grass. While she was throwing up, she could hear Morrison on the radio explaining to their sergeant that they'd found another 'omidge stiff.'

When the reveille began, the baroness immediately sat upright. Anastasia was stretching beside her. Fearfully, she looked vainly for the person she was afraid would be no longer there. 'Has anyone seen Hortense?'

'She must be in the bathroom,' said Truss, looking at the space beside him.

The baroness jumped out of bed and went outside, checked the bathroom and kitchen, called 'Hortense' and stuck her head back inside the bedroom. 'I can't see her.'

Visibly panicking, everyone tumbled out of bed. It took only a minute before they all stopped looking and collapsed onto the sofas.

'He's killed her,' said Pringle. 'That's two gone. Why didn't we notice?'

'The drinks must be spiked,' said Briggs. 'Or they're piping some kind of soporific gas into the bedroom to put us under.'

'We can't sleep there again,' screamed Marilyn.

'We'll have to, hon,' said Herblock. 'It's that or the Albanians.'

'So we just go into a gas chamber knowing that if we wake up in the morning, another one will be gone.'

'The thing is not to panic,' said the baroness. 'We don't know what happened either to Hortense or to Jake. It's really very unlikely that they came to harm.'

'She's right,' said Anastasia. 'We've got to try to keep cheerful and hope for the best. No point in moping. I'll get washed now and put the kettle on.'

When Pooley rang, Amiss been reading obituaries of Jake Thorogood and further information about the missing all morning. Although everyone agreed he was a fine writer and very knowledgeable about art, the newspapers were divided on the subject of Thorogood. His own paper, of course, had a whole page of hagiography along with a fine piece he had written on Rembrandt some years before. That he had almost completely changed his tune on conceptual art in the early noughties was explained as a road to Damascus experience that demonstrated his intellectual curiosity and his embracing of the new and challenging. More unkind papers hinted that his change of mind might have had to do with his association with the fashionable rich. Suggestions of corruption were only hinted at, for Fleet Street tends not to trash the dead until after what it considers a decent interval—especially if the departed is a journalist—but there were carefully-chosen photographs of him with the rich and famous who had money to burn on art.

Max Thorogood had issued a short, formal statement through his solicitors expressing shock and distress at the news, hope that the other missing people would soon be found, and asking for privacy for his family, whom he had taken away to an undisclosed location to avoid the gathering hordes. Thanks to a tip-off from a policeman, a tabloid had got hold of the current girlfriend, who put on a good performance at being grief-stricken. Since his death was such a hot topic, there was a rumour that some newspapers were rummaging around in his affairs with a view to running exposés. The tabloids were in ecstasy.

Pooley found a moment to call Amiss. 'It's grim news, Robert. Hortense Wilde's murdered and it's another *Hommage*—this time to Hirst.'

'Oh, God. Not bisected?'

'No. It was the shark. Not the cow. She was suspended in formaldehyde. Naked. Her husband hasn't got here yet to identify her, but there was no mistaking her from the photographs I've seen. But this is off the record for now.'

'And then there were eight!'

'I must rush, Robert. Sorry. I'm going to be interviewing Gervase Wilde shortly. Mary Lou's phone is off so I've left a message just asking her to call you. Can you look after her? She's already very fragile. Please nurture her.'

He left Amiss in what was now his customary dislocated state, pursuing news on the Internet, desperately wishing his wife worked in an office rather than a classroom and so was contactable, and checking his iPhone every couple of minutes in the hope of a message from Myles. It was a consolation when Mary Lou called. She was as frightened by the news as he was, but her suggestion of lunch promised trouble shared.

'This one's certainly unusual,' said the pathologist, who arrived shortly after Hortense's formal identification by her husband. 'There are no signs of trauma to the body and she didn't drown, so my guess is she was smothered. Then they wedged her mouth open so it'd stay that way after rigor set in. Then they popped her into the formaldehyde. She looks pretty good really. Even peaceful. Apart from the open mouth. Like one of those animals you'd see in a modern museum. '

'Quite,' said Pooley.

'I've never even heard of Oleg Sarkovsky,' said Gervase Wilde. 'What's he got to do with Hortense? Why would he want to

murder her? What harm could she have done to him. She is…
was just a scholar.'

'We were hoping you'd be able to tell us, Dr. Wilde. Sarkovsky
is a collector and we've reason to believe he'd fallen out with Jake
Thorogood and some of the other missing people.'

'I don't know Hortense's world that well, Inspector. I'd go
to art events with her sometimes, but we're both hard-working
academics who spend much of our spare time on research into
our own specialities.'

'Can we just talk about the people who disappeared at the
same time as she did, Dr. Wilde? I know this is a terrible time
for you, but we need all the information you can give us. We
need to stop this maniac.'

Wilde seemed shell-shocked, but he tried to focus. 'Very well.
Everything's a bit of a blur, but take me through the names and
I'll help if I can.'

'I'll start off alphabetically. Charlie Briggs.'

'Never heard of him until he went missing.'

'Sir Henry Fortune.'

'Oh, yes, I met Henry quite a few times at private views—
especially at Jason Pringle's gallery. Hortense really admired
Henry and Jason, and she'd have gone to exhibitions Henry
curated whenever she could. All those years ago, she thought
he'd been hard done by in not being given the Tate to run, but
she changed her mind when she saw how Nick embraced the
forces of progress. The man's a genius.'

'She wouldn't have had any business dealings with Sir Henry?'

'She gave lectures at some of his events abroad and she had
him a few times to give talks to students about what curating is
all about. But that would have been that. Not business in any
real sense.'

'Chester Herblock?'

'She got to know him recently. Through Jason, I think.'
He frowned. 'I think he asked her to talk to some collector he
thought needed advice.'

'You don't know who the collector was?'

'I don't. Though she did say something about his English being bad and that he seemed very ignorant and uncouth.'

'So it could have been Sarkovsky?'

'I suppose it's possible.'

'What kind of advice was she giving?'

'I think Herblock was his art consultant and whoever it was wanted to buy something Herblock thought he shouldn't. He brought in Hortense to point out the limitations of the artist.'

'What artist?'

'I don't know. There were quite a lot of artists of whom Hortense disapproved. She is...was...an international expert on post-colonialism and masculism in European art.'

Pooley repressed the urge to say, 'There's no answer to that,' and instead asked: 'Anastasia Holliday?'

'She knew of her through Jason and she admired what she knew of her innovative art. I think they met when Jason took Holliday to a lecture of Hortense's.'

'Marilyn Falucci Lamont?'

'I never heard her mention that name.'

'You've talked about Jason Pringle. Jake Thorogood?'

'Funny, that. She usen't to think much of Jake as a critic. He was initially terribly stuck in his attitudes, no concept of cultural theory, talked up what he should have moved beyond and was shockingly resistant to the YBAs, so they didn't get on. But he improved a lot in the last few years and they had a rapprochement.'

'Lady Troutbeck?'

'We met her once at our neighbour's. Frightful reactionary. It's a terrible thought that my poor Hortense probably spent her last days on earth in the company of such a ghastly, rude philistine.' His eyes glistened with tears. 'This is very upsetting for me, Inspector. Are we nearly finished?'

'Just Gavin Truss to go, Dr. Wilde.'

'Well, of course she and Gavin were great friends and allies at the cutting-edge of the avant-garde. Both—like me—were intellectually formed in the crucible of the Frankfurt School.'

'Sorry, sir. Could you elaborate?'

'The Frankfurt School, Inspector. Surely you know about the Frankfurt School? The *fons et origo* of critical theory. That is where Hortense and Gavin and so many others learned that Western culture is a culture of domination that must be challenged and replaced. When Gavin became principal, he got rid of the terrible dinosaur who was Professor of Fine Art and gave the job to Hortense. She proved magnificent in making the college a pioneer in popularising postmodern discourse. Good heavens, you know they used to think the importance of art was that it was decorative?' He shook his head and gave a little laugh. 'Hortense taught her students the great truth that what matters is significance.'

'You mentioned that Mr. Herblock wanted her to talk to a collector. Would that be unusual? Would she normally have much to do with collectors?'

'No. Hortense was not attracted by the social side of the art world or by rich people. As I said, she was a true scholar.' He smiled proudly. 'Someone once described her as a Robespierre among art historians.'

'And she saw that as a compliment?'

'Of course. Hortense was a woman of great integrity. Once she learned from masters like Jacques Derrida and Michel Foucault that the imperative was to replace any epistemological foundation for art history by focussing on the processes of cultural transformation, she was on a crusade.'

Pooley felt a devil rise in him. 'A crusade, sir? An interesting choice of word.'

'Oh, my God,' said Wilde. 'How could I have used such an offensive word? I'm horrified. When I think of the seminal work Hortense was doing in exposing Islamophobia in Western art, and then I use such a term!' He buried his face in his hands.

'Don't worry, sir,' said Pooley. 'I understand. Grief can do terrible things to people.'

The baroness had thought long and hard about Sarkovsky. She had no doubt that he was now psychotic, was virtually certain he had had Thorogood and Hortense killed, but was no clearer as to why. The only hope for the survivors, she reasoned, was to keep him interested enough to stagger their deaths rather than just send in thugs with machine-guns to mow them down.

Since her natural optimism kept her believing that her friends were smart and resourceful enough to come to the rescue soon, she was intent on staving off disaster. Sarkovsky liked cruelty and had little imagination, and it had taken her idea about nude painting to stop him insisting they have gladiator fights with real swords. Nude dancing was another desperate measure which she successfully traded for his idea of forcing everyone to have intercourse with the people they obviously least fancied. 'Think Scheherazade,' she said to herself yet again. 'Keep him sweet.'

She tentatively once more raised the matter of Marilyn's billions. Surely there was some way that she could buy their safety? But once again, Sarkovsky snorted his disagreement. The thrust of his argument seemed to be that in these days of tyranny by financial regulators, a decent businessman like himself could not expect that a couple of billion could change hands for no apparent reason without anyone noticing. He was ruined in Russia and the West, he was making his arrangements to escape to South America with enough money to live comfortably, but in the meantime, he was settling scores with people who had made a fool of him. One thing Sarkovsky really didn't like, he had made plain on numerous occasions, was to be made a fool of.

'Hortense Wilde! She poisonous art person. I say Chester Herblock I want to buy art same like you and me see in Europe. I get offer good collection, quick sale. Herblock say outmoded rubbish. Not hot contemporary. I say not rubbish. And keep value. He present me that bitch whore, she agree to him, and give me stupid reasons. But everybody say she is great scholar, so I think is truth. I reject collection and that Marilyn bitch whore buys it. I buy more stuff Herblock recommends. It rubbish. Real rubbish. Very rubbish. Fault of bloody Hortense Wilde.'

'I think she probably believed what she told you.'

'If she believe, she crazy. If not believe, she bad woman. But she make Oleg appeeer stupid. Same Hirst shark,' he sniggered. 'Your idea.'

Memories of other ideas she'd had for killing artists flickered through her memory, and the baroness winced. Not for the first time, she vividly recollected some of the times she had mocked Sarkovsky. Would the time she had laughed at his shirt and he had ranted and raved and finally stormed off in a sulk count as making him 'appeeer stupid'? Mindful of the hoped-for St. Martha's bequest, she had apologised the following morning and he had muttered something about how words were a sting more wounding than guns. On this, she hadn't agreed with him then and she definitely didn't agree with him now.

Amiss was in such an anguished state that he'd contemplated the brandy bottle lustfully, but he then concluded that taking to drink at eleven a.m. was something to be done if Jack was murdered. Not when he and her friends were still hoping she might survive. 'We are not all as self-indulgent and self-absorbed as you, Plutarch,' he said. The cat opened one eye and sneered, and Amiss pushed her roughly off the kitchen table. He was still licking the blood off his calf and wondering how such a fat animal could have been so dexterous, when his phone rang.

'I've only got a minute,' said Pooley. 'And I know you'll be going out now to meet Mary Lou. I'm relying on you to steady her.'

'I'll do my best, but tell me one thing. How the hell can you transport something like that tank? It must have weighed a ton.'

'It would have required a truck with a winch, and at every stage the process would have required some very strong men. But gaining access was dead easy. They'd have been able to drive right up to the front of the building to dump her.'

'Security guards?'

'It's like prisons. They're worried about what goes on inside. Not outside.'

'No sightings, I suppose?'

'Not yet. Must go, Robert.'

'Where do you think the next corpse might be deposited?'

'Well, obviously we're thinking about that. Can't stop. 'Bye.'

'After lunch, Big Brother wishes us to dance.'

'Dance?' asked Fortune. 'What do you mean "dance"?'

'Depending on what music he plays us, we will dance appropriately. He has kindly agreed shortly to supply us with champagne to get us in the mood.'

She sat down and surveyed the diminished group. 'Can everyone dance?'

Marilyn, Herblock, and Fortune, it turned out, attended many balls and regarded themselves as decent performers. Fortune, indeed, fancied himself as a master of the foxtrot. Pringle wasn't keen, but said he could shuffle round the floor if required. Truss was so unhappy and dislocated by the loss of Hortense that he could hardly talk at all, let alone about dancing. And Briggs and Anastasia both said they knew no steps but liked to party.

'And you, Jack?' asked Briggs.

'I have been told I display *élan*, if not precision.'

'What's *élan*?'

'Zeal.'

'I can imagine that,' said Anastasia.

No one had the heart to try any more general conversation, though at various times one or two of them would get up and walk around the room. The baroness noted with some satisfaction that they avoided looking at the rotting cowhead. Indeed, the day before, when Briggs had said how much he hated it, no one had said anything except the baroness, who had quipped that it seemed Hirst was for Christmas, not for life.

When Big Brother said 'Go look hatch,' they all busied themselves ferrying its contents to be laid out on Trixie and Joleen. As they finished filling glasses and sat back, the baroness cleared her throat. 'Big Brother has given me ecstasy tablets and says we're to take one each to help us get into the spirit of dancing.'

'How do we know they're not cyanide?' wailed Truss.

'If they are,' said Briggs, 'why wouldn't we take them? If he wants to kill us, he's going to kill us anyway. If he doesn't, they're probably ecstasy. Here, shove them over here.'

The baroness passed him the box she had taken from her pocket and he and Anastasia had a look. 'They're ecstasy,' he said.

'Certainly look that way,' she said. 'Let's take them now. They won't work for a while.'

Anastasia, Briggs, and the baroness washed a tablet down with champagne and passed the box around. With only Fortune expostulating, the others all followed suit. Grumbling, Fortune finally did the same.

'There's just one other thing,' said the baroness. 'When the music starts it's the signal for us to take our clothes off.'

'I thought he might want another nuddy game,' said Anastasia.

'I am expected to dance the foxtrot naked?' asked Fortune.

'That's the deal, I'm afraid,' said the baroness. 'Shall we do it with a good grace?'

◇◇◇

'I had to choose here,' said Mary Lou. 'It's the last place I met her. She loved it.'

Amiss and Mary Lou were sitting in Covent Garden, in the snug of The Salisbury, a pub favoured by the baroness because of its Victorian fittings, its connection with one of the few British prime ministers of whom she approved, its obdurate refusal to countenance music, television, or gaming machines, its kindly staff, and a snug which at many times during the day offered total privacy.

'You're speaking of her in the past tense.'

'Oh, God, so I am. I can't sleep much and when I do I have nightmares. I guess I'm really spooked.'

'Hard not to be. Now what'll you drink?'

'A pint of Tribute.'

It was an unexpected choice from someone who normally drank either wine or Coca-Cola, but Amiss fetched two pints. 'To Jack,' he said. 'May she have a safe landing.'

Mary Lou's face creased up. 'I don't like beer much, but I had to have this. Being here is bringing it all back. She went on about the merits of various brands of real ale for ages, until she settled on Tribute. Then she got upset that I'd only have a half. "What's the matter with you, Mary Lou? You're not becoming anorexic, are you? This noble Cornish beer deserves respect. Not half measures."'

Amiss laughed. 'I can hear her.'

'So I tried to explain that I have to look good on television and that means I really can't afford to put on even an ounce. The BBC is even more fattist than ageist. When it comes to women, that is. And she said "Rubbish. No one has such an informed and trenchant interviewing style. You're irreplaceable even if you turn into one of those Red Hot Mamas."'

'She's very loyal to us, isn't she, in her own way. Not that I'm implying her assessment isn't right.'

'I hope it is, but of course they also like me because I'm relatively young, passably good-looking, and black. Which in the Beeb almost makes up for my being American.'

Her face creased up again. 'And that was when I passed on Ellis' latest warning that Sarkovsky was a real bad lot and she must have nothing to do with him. She said she wouldn't be seeing him any more and that we were all fusspots.'

'Well, we've certainly got plenty to fuss about today.' He checked his phone again. 'Still nothing from Myles.'

Mary Lou leaned forward and took his hand. 'I've started praying. Dammit, I'm an American. It's what we do. Anyway, I can't think of anything else that might help.'

He put his arms around her and hugged her tightly. A man with a camera came into the snug and took a photograph. 'So who's this you're so friendly with, Mary Lou Dinsmore? It's not your husband, is it? Boyfriend?'

She looked at his triumphant expression and burst into tears.

Chapter Eleven

The assistant commissioner was looking shell-shocked. 'Sarkovsky's not in his Knightsbridge apartment, sir,' said Milton, 'nor in any of his other residences, nor on his yacht, and in fact hasn't been seen for even longer than the ten people I believe he kidnapped. We need a warrant. Immediately. I've got the paperwork all ready.'

'What exactly are you looking for?'

'We need initially to search all his properties in case he's imprisoned them in any of them. If we draw a blank, we need to look for information on some place he might own or have rented where he might be keeping them. We need immediate access to his lawyers and accountants too and all his domestic and office employees. And we need to put an army on checking land registers plus title deeds and all the rest of it.'

'Even assuming we can persuade the judge, Jim, this could turn into an international incident. We're not supposed to upset foreigners unnecessarily.'

'We have two dead bodies, sir. At the present rate of attrition, all ten of them will be dead within a few days. I don't think we should worry too much about upsetting foreigners. Collateral damage at worst.'

'Oh, I suppose so, I suppose so. Get on with it, then.'

'Thanks,' said Milton, as he jumped from his chair. As he put his hand on the handle, the assistant commissioner called to him. 'Has it occurred to you that you might be barking up the wrong tree, Jim? Maybe Sarkovsky's been kidnapped as well. Now that would put a different complexion on things, wouldn't it?'

'I have only one tree, sir. Until I see another, I'll bark up that.'

Fortunately, Mary Lou had recovered her equilibrium quickly enough to do a deal with the photographer. In exchange for him not using the photo of her crying, she agreed to give him a quote, so the picture of Amiss hugging her was run under the headline 'JUST GOOD FRIENDS,' with a few lines about how they were comforting each other over the disappearance of their friend Battling Baroness Troutbeck. The tabloid chucked in for good measure a picture of her on Pooley's arm going into a film premiere, both of them in evening dress, with a caption underneath about her husband, dashing Detective Inspector Pooley of Scotland Yard. With another picture of her interviewing a well-known actor and some guff about her coming top of some poll or other as the sexiest egghead on TV, that was another page of that tabloid happily filled.

'It's Myles, Robert. Sorry I couldn't get back to you until now. Only just got your messages. There was no coverage in the hills. What's up? Is Ida all right?'

Amiss did a double-take before remembering that Myles was one of the very few people in the world who called Jack Troutbeck by her baptismal name. 'No, she's not, Myles. She's gone missing.'

'Tell me.'

When Amiss had finished his brief account, Myles said, 'Shit. This is serious. It's that fucking psycho Sarkovsky, of course. I warned Ida a long time ago, but she had the bit between her teeth then and was galloping ahead. And then when they fell out, she kept saying he was in a sulk and didn't want anything to do with her any more so there was nothing to worry about.'

'The ghastly thing is, Myles, that it looks as if he's been paying far too much attention to her. From what we can infer, he's kidnapped a whole collection of people she's taught him to despise and is knocking them off using methods she suggested when she was being facetious. The guy's a bit literal-minded.'

'What are the cops doing?'

'I think they're just about ready to apply for search warrants, but I doubt if that'll work. We have to assume they're in London. He can't be flying them from a distant location corpse by corpse, can he? But he's hardly going to have them imprisoned in his Knightsbridge penthouse. His butler might object.'

'Of course not. Are the cops looking at his companies to see what properties they own?'

'Yes, but from what Jim says, they're not very speedy.'

'I know a man who'll cut corners, Robert. He'll be in touch with you. We need him to find where they're likely to be. Meanwhile, I'll get someone to start pulling a rescue party together and I'll get out of Iraq as fast as I can. It won't be today, though, and I doubt if it'll be tomorrow. I don't know if you pray, but if you do, pray that she's trying to be a bit more tactful than usual.'

Milton had announced late morning that Hortense Wilde had been murdered, but because of panicking by the assistant commissioner he was prevented from describing the circumstances. However Morrison had done a secret deal with a tabloid contact that would pay him enough to expand his railway and rolling stock to include Eurostar, so the news of a corpse outside the Tate was on the Internet by early afternoon. A member of the public who had been passing Tate Modern at three thirty a.m., and who had surreptitiously taken a photo of police carrying a tank to a police van, saw the news item and called another tabloid. So it was that by mid-afternoon the jigsaw was sufficiently complete for the net to be alive with the second *hommage* murder. After a fraught meeting with the assistant commissioner, Milton was allowed to confirm that rumour was fact. The press, who had been frustrated in their attempts to find the always elusive

Banksy, were now in hot pursuit of Damien Hirst. The police were putting covert night surveillance on Tate Britain, the Saatchi Gallery, the White Cube, the Gagosian gallery and any other major locations they could think of that were strongly associated with conceptual art.

'Robert Amiss.'

'I'm Mike. Myles told me to call you.'

'Oh, thank God.'

'We don't talk here. Can you meet me in an hour in central London? I'll text an address.'

'Done.'

The phone went dead.

By the time Big Brother instructed them to take their clothes off, alcohol and ecstacy had put everyone in a better mood. There had even been some nostalgic reminiscences of dances of the past. Herblock and Marilyn had had a lovely-dovey interlude recalling their first encounter at a ball raising funds for the New York Museum of Modern Art. They stripped resignedly, the music began and immediately Anastasia and Briggs began to gyrate energetically to the electronic rhythm.

'What is this?' cried Fortune. 'I can't dance to this.'

'It's House Music, Henry,' said Briggs. 'You'll get used to it.'

'Dance now or die,' interjected Big Brother.

The baroness joined the dancers, slowly followed by all the others. Still being uncharacteristically more circumspect than anyone else about her intake of alcohol, she was the only person keenly observing the incongruity of the scene, particularly the odd movements of Fortune's stomach. But within a few minutes, like everyone else, she had forgotten about anything except the pulsating beat.

'OK,' said Mike. He and Amiss were sitting in an anonymous room in a hotel on the Strand. Mike was middle-aged, leathery, and his eyes were fixed on Amiss'. 'Now I've got the story. I've got the background. Now what else can you tell me that would help us find the bastard? I don't take kindly to anyone trying to kill Jack Troutbeck. Not just because of Myles. She's our friend too. I won't forget the speech she gave us at that dinner in the Special Forces Club before we went into Iraq.'

'I'm trying,' said Amiss, 'but I wasn't always paying attention to everything Jack said about Sarkovsky.'

'If there's one thing I'm good at, Robert, it's interrogation. Now I want you to go back to the beginning and tell me everything.'

Amiss looked at his watch. 'My wife will be home soon.'

'Tell her to get here as fast as possible. And tell Mary Lou Dinsmore the same. Yes, I know her husband mustn't know about this, so she'll have to lie. Tough. Jack's life is at stake. You may trigger each others' memories.' Amiss reached for his phone. 'And, Robert, tell them they'll be staying late. Possibly very very late.'

'Everything we're finding out about Sarkovsky is appalling,' said Pooley. 'His business seems to be in free-fall, not least because he had invested so much in a joint venture with Colonel Gadaffi. Work has stopped on the museum he was building in Russia, his London office has been closed down, and his accountant hasn't heard from him in weeks.'

'What have you got out of the accountant? Does he know anything about properties we don't know about?'

'He won't talk. He just won't talk. He's too scared.'

'Get a warrant for his arrest,' said Milton. 'I want him here first thing tomorrow.'

After about half-an-hour, Fortune stopped dancing and fell on a sofa. 'Geddyouuup,' said Big Brother.

'Can't,' croaked Fortune.

'He really can't,' said the baroness. 'He's got to have a break or he'll have a heart attack. And the same applies to all of us. Whatever you have in mind, that would be a bit of an anti-climax, wouldn't it?'

'You, Diary Room. OK, Fortune stop. All others continue dance.'

As the baroness pulled on her shell-suit, for she felt strangely embarrassed at being naked talking to Sarkovsky on her own, she wasn't the only one in the room thinking about *They shoot horses, don't they?*

Aware that she was still under the influence of ecstasy, the baroness played for time. 'I've got a really good argument planned, Big Brother, but it won't work if everyone's exhausted. What do you think? Will you let us get some sleep?'

Haggling produced the agreement that as people passed out with exhaustion, they could go back to the Emin room and rest. But a few hours later the reveille sounded and within a few minutes they were all back assembled on the sofas. The baroness looked around the crumpled group of depressed people and turned to Truss with a feigned enthusiasm. 'Now, Gavin, I've been thinking about the conversation we had about Kounellis. He had a room at the Tate courtesy of what is laughingly known as the Anthony d'Offay bequest. Now will you or someone else please tell me why the taxpayer got lumbered with paying for this? It wasn't a bequest. It was a sale.'

Outbreaks of incredulity and anger from Pringle and Truss were interrupted by Fortune, who imposed silence with a wave. 'I'll handle this.' He brought as much gravitas to bear as could a plump knight in a dirty lime green shell-suit, who had recently been seen naked dancing to acid house. 'Let us be calm. What do you know of Anthony d'Offay?'

'He's a dealer who made a fortune out of all manner of dreadful contemporary artists, collected stuff as he went—especially from his clients—had it valued at a hundred and twenty-five million quid and then out of the goodness of his heart said he'd sell the seven hundred or so items as a job-lot to the nation just for what he'd paid for them. A snip at twenty-eight million, we were told by a rejoicing art establishment. But he insists on the exhibits being displayed just as he directs. And that means what are called Artist rooms just show the d'Offay exhibits of selected artists. And they're mostly full of rubbish.'

'It was incredibly generous,' shouted Pringle. 'Nick said so.'

'Sure was. I'd have paid much more for it than that,' said Marilyn.

'Before you changed course, sweetie,' said Herblock.

'Oh, yeah. Before I changed course.'

'We are familiar,' began Fortune, 'with your closed, ignorant mind…'

'Excuse me,' said Briggs. 'It seems to me that Jack knows quite a bit. She doesn't agree with you, but you can't say she's ignorant. I'd like her to tell me about this transaction.'

'Me too,' said Anastasia.

Fortune glowered, but eventually made to his friends a 'what-can-one-do?' gesture. 'Go ahead. Trash a great man and an incomparable collection.'

The baroness thought of having another drink, exercised iron control, reached instead for water, settled herself more comfortably and began. 'We should have told d'Offay to shove off, but instead, the Tate—or Tate, as we are now required to call it to show we're cool—and the National Gallery of Scotland, who now jointly own the stuff, were abject in their gratitude and sent exhibitions round the country so the population could be elevated by—if you'll excuse the expression that seems to be a constant theme in the genre which you so revere —shit.'

'I can't stand any more of this,' shouted Truss.

'Yes, you can,' said Fortune. 'Allow her to condemn herself out of her own ignorant mouth.'

The baroness made an elaborate gesture. 'Thank you, Henry.'

'I will admit that I have not yet made it to Edinburgh to see Mr. d'Offay's worthless rubbish in the modern art gallery, but I know it includes an entire room devoted to Damien Hirst's *Away from the Flock*, which some of you mightn't know is a pickled lamb. Yep. Damien bought a lamb, he got someone to suspend it in formaldehyde, and, hey presto, the taxpayer is paying for what d'Offay thinks is destined to become a milestone of post-war art. Oh, and it's in Edinburgh rather than London because, apparently, of the ubiquitousness of sheep in Scotland.'

Truss was now so much beside himself that he was rocking to and fro with his head in hands. 'Hey, Gavin,' said Anastasia. 'Cool it. Sometimes we have to hear what we don't like.'

'Would it help if I said something nice about Hirst?' said the baroness. 'In Tat's Artist room, I saw a photograph of the artist as a young man posing laughing beside a severed head. He was sixteen and doing something original, even if it was disgusting. I am grateful that he doesn't do scatology and indeed has forborne from forcing any of his excretions on us. Or even, come to think of it, his erections—unlike Terence Koh, who under the mentorship of Charles Saatchi, stuck huge erect phalluses on Jesus and the Virgin Mary, who at the time, if I remember correctly, were in a urinal.

'To give Hirst his due, if he has a penchant for polymorphous perversity, he's keeping it to himself. Unlike other d'Offay artists, like Gilbert and George.'

'I've heard of them,' said Briggs. 'Jason was recommending me to buy some of their stuff.'

'What's in their room?' asked Anastasia.

'Rubbish by two narcissistic weirdos who do photos and montages about themselves. As the great art critic Brian Sewell—who has resisted the barbarians—put it about Gilbert and George, "these names alone are enough to make the heart of the sane man sink." However, Tat disagrees. In its view, they have sacrificed their individual identities to art and thus turned the traditional notion of creativity on its head. So at the expense of the taxpayer we look at their images of fellatio, using improbably large organs of even more improbable colours. Such works, according to Tat, demonstrate their transgression and vulnerability.'

Pringle was becoming hysterical. 'But they do. They do.'

'In my view,' said the baroness 'the pair should be taken at their own early estimation. As far as I could see, their only worthwhile work in Tat was a photograph of them with cut-out letters pinned to their chests which read "George the Cunt" and "Gilbert the Shit."'

Pringle moaned.

'To move on to the Hirst room. Apart from his rare moment of originality in having that snap taken in a morgue, everything else d'Offay had bought from him was all the old dreary derivative stuff: dead sheep, spots, skulls, pharmaceutical aids. Oh, and butterflies. Another idea pinched from someone else.'

'How can you say that?' said Marilyn. 'I bought plenty of them and I was told they were original.' She shot at Herblock what the baroness thought might be a glare. He patted her hand. 'Original in the sense that he brought his own genius to bear on the insect, hon.'

'That mountebank—though, I admit, talented mountebank—Salvator Dali was painting butterflies many years ago,' said the baroness. 'Hirst merely produced labour-saving versions by buying job-lots of real butterflies and letting them loose in a gallery or sticking them onto painted surfaces. Someone should have set the anticruelty people on him. Then an American artist called Precious started using the wings of real butterflies to create the effect of stained glass windows. Ten years later, Hirst—or rather his assistants —started doing exactly the same. However, death is a big feature of the Hirst brand, and d'Offay wanted a work made specially for him, hence these unfortunate insects randomly stuck on a painting are called *Monument to the Living and the Dead.*'

'You don't get it,' shouted Pringle. 'You just don't get it. These butterflies are a metaphor for mortality. Hirst's work is about life and death: it is relevant to us all.' Then, remembering where he was, he shivered.

'Artists have always been preoccupied with life and death,' the baroness said evenly. 'It is not an original notion. We can meditate on it without having to have this sort of crap all round us to remind us. A few words would do it. May I refer you to the Book of Common Prayer: "In the midst of life we are in death.'" She looked about her and saw that she had made a tactical error: everyone was now silent and reflective. 'Oh, lord,' she said to herself. 'We're all depressed now. It's the drug wearing off.' Like an old warhorse, she stirred herself. 'But here again,' she cried, 'useless though he is, Hirst is to be preferred to Andy Warhol. Now if there was ever a charlatan who robbed the rich just for the hell of it, it was that preening, narcissistic, self-absorbed, old queen who had one good idea and flogged it to death cynically.' She saw Fortune stirring into angry life and settled back to up the ante.

It was after two a.m. when the three friends got back to the flat. 'I know we're exhausted,' said Mary Lou, 'but we've got to get our story straight for Ellis. I've already lied that I had to stay over because Rachel and I had so much work to do on my school presentation. Now let's perfect the next lie.'

Rachel gave her a sympathetic squeeze. 'It's simple enough, isn't it? We've been up late talking about Jack and wondering if there was anything useful we might have forgotten. And Robert just remembered the Albanians.'

'You call him, Mary Lou, and then you can put me on.'

She pulled her phone out of her bag. 'I hate doing this. I absolutely hate it. Ellis and I have never had to lie to each other.'

Amiss gave her a hug. 'I know, but we have to protect him and this is the only way. I'll go on lying about not having heard from Myles. You have to lie about tonight. And at least we're telling him something useful.' He laughed bleakly. 'Late in the day.'

Rachel glared at him. 'Robert, you are not to beat yourself up because you didn't think of the bloody Albanians earlier. It took three hours intense questioning for it to surface.'

'And Ellis couldn't have done what Mike did,' said Mary Lou. 'He's obviously been at this for years. I feel sucked dry.'

Rachel gave Mary Lou another squeeze. 'Robert and I will go to bed now and leave you to ring Ellis. Try not to feel bad. You're doing this for Jack.'

Milton had taken pity on Morrison and Byrne and given them a night off. They wouldn't have found the next *hommage* anyway, since it was much further down the Thames than their beat. Placed outside the O2 arena in Canary Wharf, at a cursory glance, it looked like a statue, so no one noticed it until about four a.m., when a security man having a quick cigarette spotted the notice. 'It's another of those *hommages*,' he told the police. It says "*Hommage* to Koons. Jason and Bubbles." I don't know if it's a novelty statue or they're dead people. The small fat one's sitting on the tall thin one's lap and they're wearing golden suits, golden wigs, and their faces are pasty but their lips are red. The small one's even got a little golden beard. I tell you, I've seen some strange things in my time, but this isn't something you'd want to see before breakfast.'

Having kissed Rachel goodbye and cleared the breakfast dishes, Amiss went out to the newsagents and bought all the papers. 'You interested in these 'omidge murders?' said the newsagent.

Amiss nodded. 'It's because I write crime novels,' he said. 'We have to keep an eye on real-life murders.'

'That was weird, putting that woman in that glass box like that bloke Damien Hirst put that shark. Who do you think's behind it, then?'

'No idea. Some lunatic.'

'If you ask me it's an art-lover,' said the newsagent, guffawing. 'Someone making one of those artistic statements of the obvious. Like that modern art's all baloney.'

'Maybe.'

'Mark my words, there'll be more. You've got a serial killer here. He's going to knock off all those people he kidnapped, one by one.'

'I hope you're wrong.' Amiss smiled wanly and went home.

The security man had always longed for his fifteen minutes of fame, preferably accompanied by riches, and to that end he had melted into the background once the police arrived and had called his favourite tabloid to offer an exclusive. So it was that Amiss knew there were two more *Hommage* murders before Pooley had even had time to ring him. Amiss had had promised to awaken Mary Lou at nine. It was only a quarter past eight, but he roused her anyway, told her there were things to discuss that wouldn't wait, and had coffee and toast ready for when she joined him five minutes later.

Her reaction to the news of the double murder verged briefly on the hysterical. 'Oh, Robert,' she sobbed. 'We're going to be too late. You know we are. There just isn't time to find her. And if he's now killing them in pairs, even if she lasts till the end, there are only two days to go. What are we going to do?'

'There's only one thing we can do, Mary Lou. Or, rather, one thing you can do.'

When she realised that Fortune and Pringle were both missing, the baroness had also had difficulty in staying calm. First up, she retreated into the bathroom. She went over and over what she'd said when required the night before to say who was worst. She'd definitely gone for Fortune, but she might have said something disparaging about Pringle too. 'No, no,' she told herself as she climbed out of the shower. 'It was because they were a couple. And a couple of gays at that, which of course always offended that homophobic shit. So maybe it won't apply to Chester and Marilyn.' She allowed herself to wonder if they'd be better off going on strike and daring him to send in the Albanians. Wouldn't a quick death be for the best? And then she thought of Anastasia gamely trying to be cheerful and suppressed the thought. Maybe even now Milton and Pooley had located the prison and were at the head of a task force of armed cops, all ready to take on Sarkovsky's revolutionary guard.

The image didn't give her much comfort. Whatever way she imagined it, a lot of people were likely to end up dead. And she couldn't see how the six remaining prisoners would be exceptions.

Still, her job was to rally them. Before, no doubt, having to pick yet another fight.

She dried herself, put on her soiled pink shell-suit, and went out to try to convince five terrified people that their fears were exaggerated.

◇◇◇

The commissioner was back and beside himself with frustration. 'My God,' he screamed at the assistant commissioner. 'What took you so long? We should have been in there tearing Sarkovsky's life apart two days ago. I want every member of Murder Squad on this job right now. And I want all our armed response units and firearms officers ready to go at a moment's notice. Where's Milton?'

'Interviewing Sarkovsky's accountant to see if he might know anything about any other properties the guy owns in London. But since he could have bought them through a foreign company, it won't be straightforward. We'll have to give it time.'

The commissioner, who had always hated and despised the assistant commissioner as a lazy, incompetent, buck-passing dipstick who'd only got his promotion because he was a genius box-ticker, thought of beating him to a pulp but then remembered he was a policeman and head of the Met. He clasped his hands very tightly together. 'Just get out and get on with following my instructions, Pilsworth. Now! And tell Milton to get back here as soon as possible and come to see me immediately.'

His phone rang. 'Yes, yes, yes. I'll call the Home Secretary now.'

Chapter Twelve

Pringle and Fortune had neither siblings nor living parents and with the media in full cry, a swift identification was necessary, so rather than put Allegra through it, Pooley sent for Thomas, the porter from Pringle's apartment block. 'It's not that I mind dead bodies,' he said as Pooley escorted him to the morgue. 'What with being in the St. John's Ambulance and all that I'm well used to it. But I don't like my routine being disturbed.'

'It won't take long, I promise. We'll have you back at work very soon.'

The sheets were whipped off and Thomas gazed with interest at what was revealed. 'It's Mr. Pringle and Sir Henry all right,' he said, 'but I never saw them wearing make-up before. Or wigs. Or gold suits. Or sitting on each other's laps.'

Being a man who liked to follow a thought all the way through, he added, 'Or dead, for that matter.'

'There's no evidence of any prisoners anywhere on his properties, Ellis. His domestic staff think he's still abroad. He was always very secretive about his arrangements. The warrant for his arrest has just come through so I've put out a press statement saying we urgently want him to help with our enquiries and that all information on his whereabouts would be welcome. That stupid bastard Pilsworth. We're too damn late with this.' Milton ran his hands through his hair.

'I didn't have time to tell you earlier, Jim, but we've got another lead. Robert and Rachel and Mary Lou were together last night and while talking everything over, Robert remembered a throw-away line of Jack's about Sarkovsky employing Albanians. Apparently he and Jack were talking about the characteristics of various peoples of the old Soviet Union and Sarkovsky said Ukrainian security guards were so useless he'd replaced his with Albanians. And that reminded Mary Lou that in some recent rant of Jack's she'd speculated on how long it would be before the art establishment would embrace snuff performance art. Her example was an Albanian sticking a screwdriver through his victim's cranium. I've checked this out and apparently it's their signature form of murder.'

'And?'

'And yes, Special Branch are chasing their Albanian contacts as we speak. And they're liaising with the security services too and will have the surveillance underway ASAP.'

Milton sighed the relieved sigh of a man who never failed to appreciate his luck in having a colleague he could rely on. From bitter experience he had developed the theory that in any institutional hierarchy you were doing well if two out of three in the line of command were competent. Just once in his career both his immediate superior and subordinate had been excellent at their jobs.

It was a halcyon period when no time was wasted on trying to motivate the lazy, clear up after others' mistakes or—as now with AC Pilsworth —wheedle the blindly stubborn into doing the obvious. Pending trays were cleared and moribund cases reopened. He had time for a life outside work and his marriage flourished. In his self-pitying moments, he could measure the later slow decline in his relationship with Ann by remembering a series of colleagues whose general uselessness caused him to have to work early and late.

'Thanks, Ellis. Call me when the pathologist is ready for us.'

'I rang Mike as per your instructions,' said Mary Lou, 'and I told him everything Ellis has told me about what the Yard are doing.'

'Well done. I know how difficult this is for you.'

'I never thought I'd end up playing Mata-bloody-Hari to my own husband. But I know I've no choice.'

'What did Mike say?'

'That Myles is back, that they're all working flat out and that if they get any kind of decent lead they'll be ready to move. I hope that means what it sounds as if it means.'

'I'd have more faith in the effectiveness of Myles and his superannuated comrades than in the pride of the armed wing of Scotland Yard these days. Between the press and the human rights lawyers, the poor bastards are terrified of making a mistake.'

'I don't know what to think,' said Mary Lou. 'I've a day of ghastly meetings and the phone will be silent, but it'll be on and I'll keep checking for texts. What are you going to do?'

'For now, I suppose I'll keep reading the fucking papers and hoping for a miracle.'

'This is a weird one,' said the pathologist. 'Not that the others weren't weird too. They were smothered and then put into position on a slab until rigor mortis set in and they could be moved. It must have been hard work to keep them from slumping over during the first few hours.'

'I think our murderer probably isn't short of help,' said Pooley.

'And there's a really peculiar thing about them. There are traces of paint on the thin one's penis and the fat one's stomach. I can't think of a rational explanation for that unless it's a sexual perversion. But from my cursory look, they haven't been having sex.' He paused and thought. 'Well, penetrative sex.' He shook his head. 'Sometimes I think it's time for me to retire, Ellis. It was bad enough when it was ferrets up the bum and then when strangling yourself for kicks became all the rage, but every week there seems to some new sexual perversion. This is a young man's game.' He shook his head gloomily. 'What's been going on here anyway? Who are they supposed to be?'

'It's a pastiche of Jeff Koons' sculpture of Michael Jackson and his chimpanzee Bubbles,' said Pooley. 'The original was made out of porcelain. These two were intimate friends, and the thin one used to call the fat one Bubbles.'

'Blimey, Ellis. You've got a right one there and no mistake. Murderers aren't usually so imaginative. Any guesses as to what he's likely to do next? Or where?'

As Pooley shook his head, the pathologist laughed. 'Do you know what all this reminds me of? Those painted elephants that were all over London a couple of years ago. There were hundreds of those. It's a good thing for you this guy only kidnapped ten.'

News of the Koons *hommage* caused an uproar in the European and American press. While the general public didn't much care about art, they loved imaginative murders and the connection with Michael Jackson was a gift for the chroniclers of celebrity as well as the culture brigade. Amiss tried to keep his brain from exploding by reading obituaries of Hortense Wilde, which mostly listed impenetrable titles of obviously dreadful essays buried in journals no normal person had ever heard of. Almost all had been written by her cultural tribe.

Hortense was agreed to have been a cutting edge influence in 1973 in achieving acclaim for radical artist Mary Kelly when she displayed her son's dirty nappies in the London Institute of Contemporary Arts. For this, she had been ridiculed by reactionaries. There were those, however, who felt that much more important was the erudition as a cultural analyst that she had brought to the demolition of false gods who had been worshipped just because they could paint. Without theory, as she had explained to generations of students, there could be no understanding of art. Indeed, nothing qualified as a work of art unless it could be interpreted as such by esteemed cultural commentators.

Accused of helping foment hostility towards cultural achievement, Hortense had countered that since art was a cultural construct, no one could measure cultural achievement unless it was firmly rooted in cultural theory and had cognisance of it.

Among those wrongly thought to have been persons of some cultural achievement, it turned out, were pretty well every male artist who had ever painted a woman (sexist), or anything foreign (colonialist). Indeed any Western male artist who had ever painted anything was off bounds, owing to being a masculinist, and if they made any money, a capitalist. Hortense Wilde, thought Amiss, was clearly even more of a pill than he had realised, since what was bad she automatically called good and what was good she called bad. But that didn't mean she deserved to be murdered.

Having wrung all they could out of relatives and friends of Throrogood and Hortense, broadcasters were in seventh heaven at having those of Fortune and Pringle to go after. Having concluded quickly that voices from the art establishment lamenting the deaths of luminaries and the wickedness of subverting art to murder were becoming a bit old hat, they went after Thomas, the porter, as well as Allegra and Serafina, who were still doggedly running the Pringle gallery. Having been besieged by the press for some days, the women had become veterans. Together they fashioned a few sound bites mourning the loss to them and to art of their wonderful boss and his inspirational partner and delivered them soulfully on request to microphone and cameras and down telephones.

'Don't you wish we could say what we really thought of them, Ally?' asked Serafina of Allegra.

'It'd get us a global reputation in no time, Fina, but I guess it'd put us in the shit in the job market. Tell you what, let's just get through today, and tonight we'll buy some fizz and go to my place and get completely hammered.'

◇◇◇

Fortune's heir was Pringle and Pringle was Fortune's, which initially made it difficult to get permission to investigate their finances, but they turned out to share an accountant who, after Pooley's strong-arming, decided to be helpful. 'Fortune's affairs were pretty straightforward,' he said. 'He had a substantial income, generous expenses and earned quite a bit on the side. It was different with Pringle. He made some very lucrative deals in the second half of the noughties, but invested most of his profits in shares that have dropped way down since then. The gallery's ticking over, but only just. Then there was a big sale recently that's ended up with his lawyers. He got the money, spent it, and then couldn't deliver what he'd sold. You'll need to talk to his lawyers to get more information.'

'I don't think it matters for now to find out any more about the victims, sir,' said Milton to the assistant commissioner. 'We can, I think, guarantee that they have all annoyed Sarkovsky one way or another. May I suggest that we concentrate resources on finding him?'

◇◇◇

'Robert. It's Myles.'

'Thank God you're back.'

'Hope to Christ I'm not too late. Now, there's bad news. Mike's followed up the tip about the Albanians and it's not good, I'm afraid. The cops will get nowhere with the Zekas. They're very very bad people.'

'Who the hell are the Zekas?'

'Albanian über-thugs. They've been providing security for Sarkovsky for some time. If he's keeping these people hostage and killing them, the Zekas are right for the job.'

Amiss despairingly leaned his head on his hands and inadvertently his elbow on Plutarch's tail. The result, as he complained later to Rachel, was the transformation of his desk into Armageddon. It was a testimony to his concern for the baroness that he barely noticed the upended desk-lamp, the water spewing from the knocked-over glass, and the hundreds of pages of typescript kicked into confusion on the floor. 'Sorry, Myles. I was interrupted. Tell me more.'

'They're a dreadful family, even by Albanian standards. Albanians don't do gangs. If they did, we might get somewhere taking out the main guy and turning over the others. But they do families. They're not like the Mafia. They don't do godfathers. They're more democratic. And they don't talk or betray each other. To neutralise them we'd have to take them all out. Except for the women and children. But frankly, they're such a big family, we wouldn't know where to start.'

Amiss' liberal conscience suggested protesting. He killed it. 'Why are they so dreadful?'

'Robert, in London, the Albanian thugs are the worst. As an Albanian friend remarked to me, it's that the competition is so weak. Well, when you consider that in London we've got Triads, Somalis, Islamists, IRA throwbacks, and dozens of others groups of reprobates, that means trouble. Among Albanian gangsters, the Zekas are the tops.'

'And not at market gardening, I assume.'

'No. More at torture and murder to order.'

Amiss tried to keep his voice steady. 'So what's the strategy?'

'We know who they are. We know where some of them live. We're keeping an eye to see who might turn up at their mothers'. But we also know they're randy, drunken, and girl-traffickers, so that gives us another line of enquiry.'

'Why both of them, Big Brother?'

'You say two together. Anyway, I plan execute together.'

'Because…?

'Because they cheats and liars and homosexualists and frauds and bastards and Pringle dirty Jew.'

'Did they get a lot of money off you?' asked the baroness, trying to sound as if the conversation were normal.

'Not beeg money. It same conspiracy with Thorogood about Banksy. They think they can make Oleg Sarkovsky appeer stupid. But Pringle do bad things with Briggs additionally.'

'Like what?'

'Bidding when I bidding so I pay too beeg money. Dirty crook bastard Pringle secret talking with people and getting commissions.'

'Briggs wasn't trying to cheat you, though.'

'He plot with Pringle. He laugh behind my back. I say you, nobody make Oleg Sarkovsky appeeer stupid man.'

'What about Anastasia?'

'Pringle try trick me about her. He say me she next beeg one, but she crap rubbish con trick.'

'She's just a girl trying to earn a living, surely. She wasn't trying to trick you.'

'Hah! She same all this crap rubbish artists. They all trying cheat rich people. She example, same like Pringle for dealers, Fortune for curators, and stupid bitch whore Wilde for art history person.'

'And Truss?'

'You say me all crap begeeen with teacher. He teach students all crap good enough. He example of big rubbish teacher. All trick people.'

The baroness thought of capitalising on his unusual loquacity by asking what she had done to deserve a sentence of execution, but she knew the answer already. 'So what did you do with Henry and Jason?'

He sniggered the snigger that so grated now on the baroness that she had to exert all her will-power not to flinch. 'Joke execute. Clever. I curate. *Hommage* Jeff Koons Jackson and Bubbles.'

'That wasn't my idea,' said the baroness.

'No. My idea. I clever man. Now, you got idea make me laugh today or maybe I execute all now.'

'For today's game,' said the baroness, 'we are to divide up into three teams and sculpt each other.'

'But we can't sculpt,' said Pringle.

'This is indeed true,' said the baroness. 'For a group of people with a keen interest in art—and many of whom make a good living out of it—we are singularly short of any ability to produce anything I would call art, even if many of you might say otherwise. However, nonetheless, Big Brother wants us to have a go.'

'Are we to sculpt the head or whole body?' asked Briggs.

'The whole body.' She paused.

'Don't tell me,' said Anastasia. 'In the nuddy.'

'Oh, no. Not again. I won't do it,' said Marilyn. 'Not again.'

'Food?' said the baroness. 'If just one of us doesn't obey, there'll be no food.'

'I don't care,' she said. 'There are worse things than going hungry.'

'Or drink.'

She wilted. 'Oh, all right. In what medium are we to sculpt?'

'Play-Doh.'

'What is Play-Doh?' asked Chester Herblock.

'It's squidgy stuff kids use to make shapes with,' said Anastasia. 'It's good because it's easy to clear up afterwards. I've often helped my little sister make things with it.'

'Indignity piled upon indignity,' said Herblock. 'I need a drink.'

'So do we all,' said the baroness. 'Get a few bottles out, Charlie.'

Naked, they clustered around the vast bucket and each plucked out one of the balls of pastel and began moulding it.

'What size are these sculptures supposed to be?' asked Truss. 'We'd need a few tons of it to do life-size.'

'The idea is to do miniatures,' said the baroness. 'But Big Brother wants us to do the full body.'

'Don't know that that's possible,' said Marilyn. 'The weight of the head will squash the body unless it's fat.'

'So it would work for me,' said the baroness, 'but not for you. Let's think laterally, though. We can make the bits separately and put them together lying on their backs on the floor.'

Anastasia was generous with advice, and the group soon got the knack of squeezing the compound into shape and began to develop a sense of achievement. Watching her work on a likeness of the baroness' head, they managed with their own tasks to make a shot even at eyes, noses, and mouths. From time to time, someone refilled glasses, and, gradually, there was even the occasional drunken giggle. Briggs made a commendable attempt with long yellow slivers of dough to give his bust of Anastasia long blonde locks. The baroness attempted to adorn Truss' face with a halo of black curls. After a couple of hours, they had six reasonably complete small pink corpses stretched out on the floor. Remarking that they might be able to flog the results when they got out, the baroness licensed everyone to wash and dress.

Peace reigned even through lunch, during which the baroness assured them once again that Big Brother was a guy with a great sense of humour who was probably having a laugh with the evictees. Anastasia was equally bullish. Everyone drank a lot except for the baroness, who was awaiting the moment to foment yet another argument.

◇◇◇

Amiss was watching a scrum of photographers snapping Anastasia Holliday's parents, who had just come off the plane from Sydney. Having been pursued to the airport by a press posse, they had been greeted at Heathrow by another shrieking the news that two more of the missing had been found dead. Having been given the details, they were asked to describe their feelings.

'How do you think we're feeling, you dipsticks?' shouted Ben Holliday. 'Our only daughter's missing and your police are as useless as tits on a bull.' As he grabbed his wife's hand and began to plough through the crowd, Mary Lou rang Amiss.

'Ellis just called and I managed to keep him long enough on the phone demanding news of progress to find out that a Special Branch informant in an Albanian-owned brothel reported that some guy called Akim, one of the owners—who is also one of her regulars—was very keyed up on Tuesday night.'

'The night Jake Thorogood was killed?'

'Yep. She was surprised that he was sober, because he almost never is, but he explained that he couldn't drink because he had a very important mission. And she knows he works for a Russian, because when he's drunk he curses Russians. Apparently he didn't stick around long, looked at his watch about ten and rushed off and into his BMW.'

'He didn't say where the brothel was?'

'Just that it was north. And then he had to hang up.'

'Well done. I'll call Mike now.'

◇◇◇

'Oh, for God's sake,' shouted Gavin Truss, 'you'll be telling us next that nothing in Tate Modern is art.'

'Most of what goes on in that repugnant edifice of brutalist architecture too damn right isn't art,' said the baroness. 'Tat Modern is full of tat and is crammed to the gills with the effluence of so-called artists who couldn't draw or paint to save their stupid lives. And any good stuff they've got is doled out grudgingly and rarely.'

'It's the most successful art gallery in Europe. I suppose that counts for nothing?'

'Compare like with like. It's a bloody fairground, not an art gallery. I bet it doesn't have more visitors that the Paris Disney.'

'How can you justify that, you awful person?' shouted Truss. 'What do you mean fairground?'

'Take the Tat's turbine hall. All five stories and forty thousand square feet of it. Now Serota's empire includes vast storehouses full of great art that the public doesn't get to see. You might think he'd be glad to fill this huge space with enormous pictures and grand sculpture. At least occasionally. Henry Moore could cut a dash here. But our friend Sclerota, as I like to call him, commissions installations specifically geared to the Hall and otherwise leaves it barren.'

Marilyn was looking worried. 'What do you think, hon?' she asked Herblock. 'Maybe Jack has a point. It's a big space. Maybe it should be filled with something.'

'You might be right, hon. The longer I'm in here looking at flies and dead cows, the more I begin to think we haven't been giving Michelangelo enough respect.'

'You may,' said Truss grudgingly, 'have a point about empty spaces, Jack. I have my differences with Nick. I find him rather unimaginative. But surely even you can rejoice in the magnificence of Weiwei's majestic installation.'

'I'm lost,' said Anastasia.

'Weiwei's main claim to fame is that the Chinese government persecutes him,' said the baroness. 'Gives him no end of cachet.'

'I think she's actually evil,' whispered Truss to Herblock, who shrugged.

'Oh, I've heard of him,' said Anastasia. 'He did something with sunflower seeds, didn't he?'

The baroness began to laugh. 'That was funny.'

'Him being persecuted by his government was funny?' asked Charlie Briggs, whose brow was furrowed.

'No, no. Him being persecuted by Health and Safety.'

Anastasia was puzzled. 'What? I thought he got banged up in China.'

'Our Health and Safety, Anastasia. They're world-class. You see Weiwei produced for the Tat hall an enormous field made of a hundred million sunflower seeds. Except they weren't sunflower seeds but porcelain replicas, individually made and handpainted over a couple of years by sixteen hundred workers in Jingdezhen, which of course you'll undoubtedly know has been the ceramic capital of China for almost two millennia. I think it was supposed to remind us that many poor bastards had nothing else to eat during the Cultural Revolution. No wonder his government isn't pleased with him.

'Having cottoned on to the fact that what visitors to Tat Modern are mostly looking for is a funfair, WeiWei essentially turned a huge part of the hall into a kind of playpen. The visitors played with the seeds as they might with sand, ran them through their fingers, danced on them and rolled in them.'

'Sounds like fun.'

'It was, rather. Whether it was art was another matter, but fun it undoubtedly was. I would quite have liked a bit of a roll among the seeds myself for nostalgic reasons, but I never got the chance. It took only a couple of days for the puritans to strike. Within forty-eight hours, the installation had been roped off and the public ordered to keep outside a barrier lest dust-inhalation damage their lungs.'

Anastasia ruminated. 'What happened to the seeds after the exhibition closed?'

'Last I heard they were sold off at Sotheby's about a quarter-ton at a time. The first lot, I seem to remember, went for something like £3.50 a seed. Weiwei won't starve. Mind you, Sclerota's made off with the bulk of it for Tat at God-knows-who's expense. You can look at it, but you still won't be allowed touch.'

'You are an absolutely appalling woman,' said Truss, his every word dripping loathing. 'What about Louise Bourgeois, if you've heard of her. Would you describe her work as fit for a funfair?'

'Some of it certainly is. Funfairs love freaks.' She turned to Anastasia. 'Bourgeois deserves a bit of respect. She showed an enormous steel-and-marble spider in that hall a few years ago. It was a tribute to her mother, if I remember rightly. I don't know if they got on. Sadly, the public weren't allowed to climb up and down it.

'I admit she has some skill. Amazing that Sclerota let her into the building if you think about it.' She grunted. 'The Belgian who installed huge steel circular tubes for the punters to slide down was more his sort of thing. And someone called Doris from Columbia who beats up furniture and chucks chairs around for a living. Her contribution to the gaiety of nations was to create a five hundred foot crack across the hall. Apparently it was about racism and colonialism. It cost about £300K and almost fell victim to the health and safety police because kids tried to jump into it.'

'Why not just turn the hall into a permanent fairground?' asked Anastasia. 'Take away the health and safety people and have dare-devil attractions like a speeded-up merry-go-round or dodgems without brakes. Performance art and all that. People like me could do turns.'

She caught sight of Truss' expression. 'Just a thought,' she said, and poured out some more wine.

'Laidee Troutbeck to Diary Room.'

As the baroness reluctantly got to her feet, she tried to summon up a little gratitude that this time, at least, it wouldn't be difficult to choose.

Chapter Thirteen

To Milton's intense frustration, no one had got anywhere in the questioning of any Zekas and no one admitted to knowing anything about the whereabouts of Akim although there were suggestions he might have gone back to Kosovo for a holiday. Worse still, Akim hadn't visited Edona on Tuesday or Wednesday night. She reported on Friday that he'd called to order her to be ready and energetic about four o'clock on Saturday morning, which boded very ill.

The commissioner chaired the meeting with Special Branch and the firearms unit as they all tried to work out what to do. AC Pilsworth's suggestion that Akim Zeka be arrested and held for questioning when he arrived at the brothel was greeted with incredulity. 'You've heard what they're like,' said the head of Special Branch. 'He won't talk. It's a matter of pride. We could hold him for days and get nothing out of him. Our only chance is to follow him back to his HQ, hope the prisoners are there, and try to get them out alive.'

'If any of them are still alive,' said Milton. 'Sarkovsky knows we're after him and he must want to cut his losses and get out of the country. In fact I can't think what's kept him so long.'

There was a long and worried discussion about the difficulty of trailing Zeka from the brothel without being spotted, while having a firearms unit ready to roll into wherever he led them. One decision everyone agreed on was that since Fortune and

Pringle had been left beside the O2, there was now no point in keeping covert surveillance on the galleries.

Martin Conroy didn't pay much attention to the news, and he didn't care about the art world, but he was sorry that Jack Troutbeck was in trouble. He'd enjoyed the rousing speech she'd given a few years previously at an SAS reunion and had heard vaguely that she was close to Myles Cavendish, under whom he'd served in Iraq. Still, he was a man who concentrated on the work in hand and avoided all distractions, so it wasn't until he got home mid-evening that he looked at the news and saw that the police were looking for Oleg Sarkovsky in connection with the *hommage* murders.

By instinct and by training, Conroy avoided impulsiveness, so rather than immediately ring the police, he gave himself a couple of minutes to think. Then he looked up his private book of phone numbers and called Cavendish. After their conversation, Cavendish immediately called Mike Rogers and gave him the address. 'I told him not to tell the cops. This is no time to piss about. There's no way the cops could get into that house without Sarkovsky knowing, and if Sarkovsky knows, he'll kill her and the rest of them. We've got to get in there now and without him knowing. I've texted the others with the code.'

'OK. I'll be on my way there in ten.'

Rogers dressed in his discreet combat gear, loaded his boot with a small arsenal and went ahead to suss out the house Conroy had identified. Within a few minutes of locating it, he had parked, put on a balaclava, selected a gun and a sharp knife and had slipped onto the site. He was in his element doing the job that for over thirty years—in the army and working privately—had given him his greatest thrills.

As he circled cautiously around the bank of portacabins, he was almost caught by the lights of the truck that came out of a garage at the back and drew up a couple of feet from him, but he slunk into the shadows just in time behind a half-built wall. And so it was that he had an excellent view of six large men coming out of a doorway carrying between them what looked like a cross and a corpse. When the truck and the van had driven away he made a call to Cavendish.

Followed by a nondescript white van, the brown flat-bed truck festooned with the livery of Westminster Council drove from Cockspur Street into Trafalgar Square, took an abrupt left, drove past the fountain and parked beside the empty plinth in front of the National Gallery. It was a cold night with a slight drizzle, so there were no loving couples sitting on the steps or by the fountains. There were taxis going past, the odd bus and a few pedestrians, but, apart from the inebriates who were trying to decide where to go next, people were mostly rushing home.

Two men dressed in oil skins with 'Westminster Council' in large letters got out of the truck and were joined by four more from the van. They hauled grey barriers from the back of the truck and put them all around the plinth, blocking all access. They then took out a ladder and extended it until it reached over twenty feet to the top. Three of them climbed up.

A passerby became curious enough to come down the stairs and lean over a barrier. 'What are you doing?' he called to the nearest workman.

'We're putting up a sculpture on the plinth for the opening tomorrow.'

'What's it like?'

'Ugly,' said the foreman. 'Black ugly thing.'

The passer-by shook his head. 'Bloody modern art,' he said, and wandered off.

It took them the best part of an hour to hoist the iron structure from the truck on to the plinth and secure it safely. Getting the corpse out of the van and up there was simple by comparison. Although Sarkovsky had protested, it had been decided that a crucifixion was one complication too many, so they just tied the limbs to the cross securely, lowered the winch, retrieved the ladders and barriers and got back in the vehicles.

They had just driven out of the square when Vernon Morrison and Sarah Byrne entered it from the Strand.

Morrison was even more fed-up than usual. 'I tell you, Sarah, I don't know why we put up with this. What good are we doing walkin' around and round in the rain only gettin' our death of cold? More and more I begin to think I'll have to pack this job in. It's all right for all those wankers sitting comfy in their offices orderin' us about. And now they're talkin' of fitness tests. Fitness tests? What the fuck? At my age am I supposed to be brawn or brain?'

'I thought we did something useful with those drunks in Charing Cross Station, Vernon. Defused a potentially bad situation, don't you think?'

'You may think so. I still think we should have arrested them.' He looked at his watch. 'We could go back to the station now.'

'Let's just give it another five minutes, Vernon. We're supposed to go round the square. Let's just do that. With everyone in a state at the moment, we don't want to give Sarge any excuse to bawl us out.' Grumbling, he acquiesced. They walked past St. Martin's in the Fields with only the briefest of comments from Morrison about how the bloody vicar let down the neighbourhood by running a doss house, then crossed the street to the pedestrianised area. As they walked past the National Gallery, Byrne looked to her left. 'What's that, Vernon. On that plinth?'

'What do you think? Another statue of some military nob. Like on the other plinths.'

'Yes, but there isn't supposed to be anything there. It's the fourth plinth that has different sculptures at different times. Didn't you see they've decided to put something cheerful up for the Olympics. A kid on a rocking horse, I read. This one looks more like the black sculptures on those other plinths that are supposed to be old-fashioned.'

They crossed over. 'This is something horrible, Vernon. I can't see what it is properly, but it looks to me like a man in uniform on a cross.'

'Are you saying it could be another hommidge?'

'I am.'

'Oh, Gawd. What have we done to deserve this?'

Morrison went on grumbling as Bryan pressed the red button on her radio. Inwardly, however, he was thinking that he'd had another bit of luck. Reinforcements would be here in a minute, and once he was sure it was another hommidge and enough cops were on the spot so no one could finger him, he could find a minute to phone that helpful journalist. Hadn't she told him to call her anytime he had any information. He went down the steps to find a suitable place and saw the big white label saying: 'NAZI JESUS—*HOMMAGE* TO THE CHAPMANS'.

The four Zekas in the van were in high spirits on the way back to north London. None of them had been enjoying this job much because they hated being stuck in the bunker. Akim had told them that the boss had had big plans for it. The room the prisoners spent the day in was to have been a great ballroom. He'd had the staircase down to it decorated the way he liked so as to give the prisoners a good impression before landing them in the horror room. Everyone thought it funny when they saw how shocked they all were when they saw that.

But for weeks now the Zekas had been fed up and uncomfortable in what was no better than a building site and they were overjoyed to think they'd soon be released. They didn't get the point of all the work that had gone into constructing peculiar decorations from pictures, but they didn't care. If the boss wanted them to furnish rooms with disgusting things, or prepare strange deaths for people, that was OK with them. Better than ditch-digging, as Akim constantly reminded them. They had a couple of craftsmen among them who got a kick out of it and fortunately Diran had an artistic streak so painting corpses wasn't a problem.

Having to spend hours listening to and watching the prisoners had bored them senseless except for the good moments when that blonde was skipping around with no clothes on. The optimists among them hoped they might have a chance to screw her before they topped her, and Akim had promised that if there was time they could all have a go. There had been debate as to whether anyone one fancied doing it to the old women, and a few had said they wouldn't mind.

They hadn't been allowed out at all—except to strew corpses around London—and they resented it that Akim always got to go to the shop and the take-aways and that he'd even been allowed a visit to the brothel when their needs were just as great. But Akim was Akim, and they did what he told them.

The Zekas didn't like the boss. Apart from a couple of new-comers, the Zekas mostly had excellent English, but the boss was crap. Those who had done a bit of security work for him over a couple of years in London said he was OK most of the time, but that when he got angry he was a maniac and he got angry if you misunderstood an order and said you were stupid even though it was him that couldn't learn the language.

The boss hadn't left the bunker since the kidnappings began. He stayed in his room a lot of the time, he talked to the fat woman sometimes, he spent hours in the room with the screens watching the prisoners—even when they were just talking—but it was the Zekas who had to watch all round the clock in case anyone tried to escape and they had to shoot them.

And then there had been all those strange killings. The Zekas didn't have a problem with killing: it was part of their stock-in-trade. But all this business with balloons and tanks and funny clothes was not what they were used to. And, indeed, being Muslim, they worried in case their mothers found out about the crucifix and thought touching it haram. The boss was a bit of a pervert, they'd concluded, and while they'd nothing against perverts if they paid for their perversions, what he made them do was hard work. That last carry-on shaving that little guy and blacking him up had been almost as creepy as the business the night before with the two queers. And although they were hazy about their history and weren't quite sure what the Zeka position was on the Second World War, they thought it weird to be dressing up a corpse as a Nazi.

Zekas were proud professionals and none of them would let down the family, so they accepted the risks of the job, but none

of them wanted to end up dead or in jail, so they were very happy
to have been promised that it would be all over by the middle
of the morning and they could go back home with money for
all the raki and girls they could consume.

Akim's phone rang as they passed Regent's Park. 'Yes, boss…
yes, yes, all OK. We'll be back soon…What…Why…Straight-
away?...Oh, OK…OK…OK.' He hung up, furious that he
would not be enjoying Edona this night, and called his brother,
who was driving the van. 'OK, Diran, change of plan. Boss
wants to leave the country this morning so we've got to kill the
others when we get back.' He brushed aside the grumbles about
overwork and tiredness. 'It's easy. Won't take us long. First we
lock the bedroom, then we open box, collect prisoners from the
bedroom, put them in the chairs and slit their throats. Close
box again. Put on label saying *"Last Orders"*. Easy.'

'Ugh! Flies. Horrible.'

'We have protective headgear. We'll be fine.'

'Will there be time for rape?'

'I'll have to check with the boss about timing. But maybe
with a bit of luck.'

'Do we all leave when they're in the case?'

'Boss wants an hour to watch flies get to work. Then we can
leave and take him to plane. We must stay with him in case of
nosey cops. When he's gone we'll sleep, and then tonight we'll all
have a big party with the girls.' Diran grunted unenthusiastically.
'Tell you what. We'll have fireworks too. Tell them.'

The contingent in the van initially reacted as Diran had,
but soon he could reassure Akim that the promises had made
everyone happy. Akim thought of calling Edona to tell her not
to stay up for him, but then he decided not to bother. Waiting
and fucking, that's what prostitutes were for. Treat them too well
and they might forget their place.

◇◇◇

Not only did Amiss know he wouldn't be able to sleep; he knew
there wasn't any point in even trying. And anyway he didn't want
to. He had persuaded Rachel to go to bed, promising to wake

her immediately if there were any news. Mary Lou rang about eleven to report that what sounded like half the Metropolitan police force would be spread around north London in the early hours following an Albanian from a brothel. When she had told Mike Rogers he had thanked her monosyllabically. 'Do you think Myles and his guys have anything up their sleeves, Robert?'

'I can't think what they'd have, Mary Lou, but I won't be surprised if they come up with something.'

'I'm so confused. I think my husband's wonderful, I have great admiration for Jim, but I really haven't got much faith in the police. That asshole Pilsworth just set up obstacle after obstacle after stupid obstacle. Oh, hell. One way or the other, Ellis is going to be out all night, probably chasing shadows.'

It took only a minute to persuade her to pack her tooth-brush and come over. For the next few hours they watched news channels, which offered interviews with distraught people from the art world and so-called experts droning on about kidnappings and hostage-releases they had known. From time to time Amiss took stock on his computer and tried to make Mary Lou laugh by reading out particularly ludicrous extracts from appreciations of Fortune and Pringle. Now that he was dead, and was no longer a competitor, European curators had queued up to be interviewed about the breadth and depth of Fortune's cosmopolitanism. He was a curator who refused to be bound by national or cultural barriers. There was, apparently, nothing Little Englandish about Henry Fortune—unlike, they were implying, his London-based equivalents.

'Heaven forfend that at a time when Jack Troutbeck is in mortal danger I should say anything good about Sir Nicholas Serota,' said Mary Lou. 'But when I listen to these patronising tossers implying that what happens on the Continent trumps what happens in London, I want to confront them with the simple fact that even if the contemporary art here is crap, at least people are trying to do something. The French don't even bother any more. They just live off the past. Like the Italians.'

And so, with periodic lapses into invective, nostalgia or frightened speculation, the two friends whiled the hours away.

Now happy about another successful foray and the promise of celebration to come, and geared up to murder five people who would not pose a problem, the four Zekas were quite cheery as they were deposited at the entrance to the basement. Not until the key had turned in the lock and the burglar alarm been disabled, did four men in balaclavas emerge from the shadows, stick knives in the backs of their necks and push them through the door. They were joined in short order by Akim and Diran, both with knives pressing on their necks. Four other men with covered faces stood watching from the sidelines, and a small man stepped forward and asked: 'Who's the leader?'

No one said anything.

'Tell us, or we'll kill one of you at random,' he said. 'And we mean it. We are SAS.'

Five Zekas looked imploringly at Akim, who stepped forward. 'OK. I'm leader.'

'That's good to know. Now, this is what I want you to do.' Cavendish beckoned to Rogers, who showed his machine gun. 'You see, we're not just SAS, Mr. Zeka. These people are our family, Mr. Zeka. We feel about them as you do about yours. Now listen to me, tell me what I want to know and do what I say, or you'll all be dead. And you won't die slowly.'

Milton and Pooley were so occupied with last-minute details for what was informally known as 'Brothel Watch' that they didn't have time even to take five minutes out to leave the Yard to look at the fourth plinth. What mattered to them—but what they didn't admit except to each other—was that the corpse was male. Both of them were tormented by the fear that now Sarkovsky knew the police were after him, he might stop dragging out the killings and see everyone off at once. All they had was the brothel tip, so they were giving it everything they had.

They were furious, though, when it hit the wires that there was another *hommage* murder and that, amazingly, the corpse was displayed right in the centre of London, less than a mile from the mighty Scotland Yard. Even at that time of the morning, there were angry commentators complaining that there should have been surveillance on such an obvious target as the plinth and the National Gallery. The police remained tight-lipped about what they had removed from the plinth, but Morrison's leak got the media going on the Chapman Brothers and their *Fucking Hell* exhibition about Jesus and Nazis.

The Cavendish crew, as they liked to describe themselves, had an unexpectedly easy time. Akim Zeka was no quitter, but he was a realist, and he could see no way out. If these guys were family, they were serious. They had already shown that they knew what they were doing, and he knew from the way the little guy talked that he wasn't bull-shitting.

Akim didn't enjoy the idea of ending up in jail, but he even less wanted to be dead and even less than that did he want his mother cursing him because he'd left her short of a couple of sons and several nephews. The British were mad, so even if they had to go to prison, they'd be out in ten or fifteen years. Edona would be past it then, but there would be others.

'OK,' he said. 'What do you want?'

Half-an-hour later, a small man opened the door of the Emin bedroom, switched on the light, went over to a snoring, smelly figure, shook her and whispered, 'Ida.' The baroness woke instantly and put her arms around him. 'Ssssh, Ida. Come outside.'

He helped her out and hugged her.

'I knew you'd get here in time, Myles. I didn't know how. But I knew you would.'

'Gavin Truss is gone too, but the rest of you are safe.'

'Are the evictees dead?'

'Fraid so. Now I have to go, Jack.'

'Go? What do you mean, go?'

'I just wanted to tell you you're all safe and the police will be along shortly when we tip them off. But we need to get away. You don't want me to land in jail, do you?'

'Sarkovsky?' asked the baroness.

'You sound nervous.'

'Nervous? Yes, for once, I admit to being nervous.'

'He's dead.'

'The Albanians?'

'Securely locked up. Now you need to go back to bed and stay there until the cops arrive. Then you act surprised. I'll be disappearing again for a while but I'll be in touch when I can. And, of course, you won't mention you've seen me.'

The baroness gave the only real laugh of the week. 'As if I would, Myles. As if I would.'

Mary Lou fell on her phone so enthusiastically that she pressed the red button by mistake, but before she could cry with frustration, Pooley rang again. The call was short and Mary Lou almost collapsed after it. 'She's definitely alive,' she told Amiss, as she began to cry. 'He's seen her. The police got an anonymous tip-off to search the basement of a huge house in Hampstead, they found the door open, five survivors, several Albanians bound, gagged, and locked in, and a dead Sarkovsky.'

'And no superannuated SAS people?'

'Certainly not. Why should there be any?'

'Jack has always instructed me to be an optimist,' said Amiss. 'That's why I keep champagne in the fridge. Open it and I'll wake Rachel.'

Chapter Fourteen

It was a week after the rescue and Pooley and Mary Lou were at home having their first evening alone since the baroness had first disappeared. 'I'm only just grasping that it's all over,' she said. 'I feel almost normal. And I can't wait to see her tomorrow night. It's a pity you can't be there.'

'I'd love to be at her dinner, darling, but she'll understand why Jim and I should stay away from her for the moment until it's all blown over. She's still being papped wherever she goes and there are a lot of unanswered questions we don't want anyone to ask us.'

'She understands, hon. I'll be going in and out the back door of ffeatherstonehaugh's so it'll only be Robert and Rachel they'll be able to photograph.'

'Myles?'

'Yes. You know Robert wasn't able to reach him until after the whole drama was over but he finally got back from Iraq this morning.'

Pooley leaned across the debris of the celebratory dinner Mary Lou had ordered in and took her hand. 'You remember we always agreed to have no secrets from each other?'

'I do.'

'So I should confess that I checked the texts on your phone and found one that was incriminating.'

'What did it say?'

'"She's OK."'

'That was it? Doesn't sound very incriminating to me.'

'It was sent about five minutes before we had the tip-off about where to find them.'

'Did you check the number?'

'No. I deleted it. Besides, I'm sure that number is no longer obtainable.'

'Are you asking any questions?'

'I'm not. I've been able to tell my superiors that I know nothing about who the rescuers were. I'd like to keep it that way. We made a balls of the entire investigation and some mysterious people didn't. I just wanted you and Robert to know that I'm not a mug. And that I understand why and what I don't know. In fact, to misquote Donald Rumsfeld, you might say it's a known unknown.'

'What happened to my correct policeman?'

'Even correct policemen have feelings and understand moral dilemmas.' He leaned over and kissed her.

Even by her standards, the baroness was dressed exotically. Her crimson silk robe had a deep purple lining and after she had greeted Amiss and Rachel she turned around and displayed the large yellow dragon climbing up her back. 'After wearing a stinking shell-suit for what seemed like years, I had to get something to obliterate the memory,' she told them, as she waved them to seats between Cavendish and Mary Lou, handed them glasses and settled in the empty chair between them.

'To the Marines,' she said. 'And to those who sent for them.'

'Keep it discreet, Ida.'

'That's why I got a private room, Myles. I promise to be careful when the waiters are here.'

'I genuinely have only just arrived here from Iraq,' he said. 'I've been in and out illicitly, so my passport shows I've been there all along. Now what's been happening?'

'The Albanians have all pleaded guilty but presumably their lawyers will come up with mitigating circumstances,' said Mary Lou. 'Anyway, with Sarkovsky dead, it's pretty well all over. No one has a clue who were the mysterious rescuers who got there before the police and never took their balaclavas off. And no one's mentioned you.'

'And Sarkovsky?' asked Cavendish. 'How do they think he died?'

'Looks as if he blew his brains out, Myles,' said the baroness.

'That's the view of the pathologist, Ellis tells me,' said Mary Lou.

'That seems satisfactory, then,' said Cavendish. 'From what I've heard, the chap was in a tight spot. He probably felt he had no option.'

'Though of course there is a school of thought in the liberal press that thinks he was a victim of some rogue paramilitary outfit.'

The baroness snorted. 'You mean the human rights lawyers are looking to get in on the game?'

Mary Lou smiled seraphically. 'Maybe if Sarkovsky had anyone that cared about him there might have been a case to pursue, but no one does. He was effectively bankrupt, his ex-wives hated him, and his children are indifferent.'

'Was he really bankrupt?' asked Rachel. 'Wasn't he supposed to be taking off for South America? Presumably he had plenty of money there.'

'I have a friend who works in Inland Revenue,' said Cavendish. 'He tells me that it's fruitless trying to track down money in South America. Now tell me, what's happened to your other companions in tribulation?'

'Anastasia's gone back to Australia with her parents, taking Charlie with her. Since they got out, they've had a torrid week in the Dorchester, since Charlie decided it was time he spent his money in a way he would enjoy. As Anastasia confided to me, even in the depths of the chamber of horrors, she quite fancied the idea of him putting his roaring roger into her laughing tackle.'

She took another draught. 'I do like Anastasia. Anyway, Charlie's resigned from his job, asked his sister to sell his art collection and is going to give some months to thinking what to do with himself. She's doing the same. After all, she explained, when you've come within a bee's todger of death, it changes your outlook. Her parents are ranchers; she thinks maybe that's the way to go. She's decided he needs taking in hand and she should probably marry him though she hasn't told him yet. But I'm proud to say that I'm to be Matron of Honour.'

'So the experience has been good for them,' said Amiss.

'Indeed. Even if it wasn't much good for the rest of us, particularly the dead ones. I doubt if the lives of Marilyn and Chester will be drastically altered. They know only one world. Although I doubt if Marilyn will ever again put money into conceptual art. She is, however, I'm pleased to say, giving a considerable gift to St. Martha's.'

'Because?'

'Because a kindly policeman called Ellis Pooley mentioned that an Albanian had said they'd all have been dead three days earlier if it hadn't been that the fat woman made Sarkovsky want to watch them play games and have arguments.'

'You mean you weren't to be knocked off night after night?'

'Apparently not. He had a grand plan for emulating Anthony Gormley by having figures appear all over London on the same day. But then my suggestion of games got the better of him.'

'What do you mean figures all over London? Weren't the last of you to be seen off in that fly box?'

'That was a last-minute substitution. The head Albanian said he had planned some sort of porn Koons death for Anastasia and Charlie. I was to be the *pièce de resistance*. Hirst's golden bull. In a glass tank, on all fours with a gilded head, hands, and feet.'

'And Marilyn and Chester?'

'History doesn't record.'

The door opened, and the head waiter arrived. 'Lady Troutbeck,' he said. 'I just want you to know that the staff of ffeatherstonehaugh's are all delighted that you are safe and well.'

The baroness stood up and bowed. 'Thank you, Vittorio. I appreciate that sentiment. And I'm sure they have outdone themselves to ensure that we have a good dinner tonight.'

◇◇◇

'Thank God it's Friday,' said Rachel, as she finished the fifth course and the sixth glass of wine and leaned back exhausted in her chair.

'Of course you're the only one among us who keeps regular hours,' said the baroness. 'Good. Now you'll be able to drink some port.'

'First,' said Amiss, 'I want to propose another toast with whatever you have in your glasses. To Rachel and Mary Lou, for triumphing over the forces of educational darkness yesterday!'

Mary Lou's visit to Rachel's school had been an uproarious success. The murders had coincidentally put art so centre-stage that the entire school attended her presentation. According to Rachel's account, Mary Lou had excelled herself. She had shown them conceptual art from every angle and persuaded them to laugh at it. She had shown them slides of the Sistine Chapel and told them of Michelangelo's struggles with the sheer physical challenges. She fascinated them with several Rembrandt self-portraits along with stories of some of tribulations he faced in his private life and enchanted them with his *Lion Resting*. Along with some Van Goghs, she told them of how his mental problems brought about suffering and finally his suicide. She told them simply the story of Icarus, showed them Breugel's *Landscape with the Fall of Icarus* and read them Auden's poem.

Then she spoke about home-grown genius, told them of Stubbs' anatomical dissections and how they had enabled him to produce *Whistlejack,* and of Turner's life of experimentation with illustrating such intangibles as weather and light. *The Fighting Temeraire* elicited oooohs and aaahs and led her into talking of the Turner Prize with a few choice specimens of winning entries that got them all scoffing.

Finally, she told them the story of the emperor's new clothes and told them that grown-ups and clever people could be very silly and that they should trust their own judgement. 'And the result,' said Rachel, 'was a demand from the kids to be taken to see what they called "real" paintings and a promise from their now very own celeb that she'd go with them. The head and several of the teachers were furious, but they've had to cave in.'

When the acclamation had died down, and to the baroness' delight, everyone was drinking port, Rachel asked her question. 'There's something really bugging me, Jack. I looked up the most famous names that have come up in all these discussions, and far too many of them are Jewish for my comfort. I had a look at the ArtReview Power 100, and it's laden with Jewish curators and dealers and critics and collectors. It's only the artists who are mostly gentiles.'

'Good grief,' said Amiss. 'You didn't tell me this. It's another international Jewish conspiracy.'

'I know we get blamed for everything from the killing of Jesus to the collapse of the financial markets,' said Rachel. 'And I'm inured to that. But is conceptual art really our fault?'

'Stuff and nonsense,' said the baroness. 'You're being wet, Rachel. You know perfectly well Jews are smart, disputatious, and free-thinkers, and what with being persecuted everywhere they go for those reasons, their skills tend towards the portable. Like ideas and finance and the arts.'

'I know. But then I looked up even more and found the Frankfurt school that started all this cultural relativist nonsense was dominated by them.'

'Look here, Rachel. It's called swings and roundabouts. You buggers are obsessed with education and art, you never stop thinking and arguing and sometimes you get it wrong but mostly you give us great scientists and musicians and thinkers that have a disproportionate effect on business and finance because you're so bloody brilliant.

'Although I think the Irish are up there with you when it comes to being good company—and, unlike you, they understand the attraction of alcohol—you are the most entertaining, funniest, warmest and stimulating crew on earth.'

Rachel opened her mouth and the baroness waved at her dismissively.

'There are downsides, of course. You also produce innumerable clever sillies, like Marx and Freud and Trotsky and, indeed,
Serota. Israel fights for its life as much with loud-voiced enemies
within as with Jew-haters outside. And because most people are
less clever, less successful, less perverse, and less open to new ideas
than you lot are, that gets you hated, especially by poor bastards
stuck in the intellectual rigidity of radical Islam.

'There has to be someone to blame for everything. It's your
people's burden. Live with it, stamp on your tribal propensity
for angst and guilt, however much you might revel in it. And
for Christ's sake, lighten up.'

She had another sip of port and looked straight at Rachel.
'Your choice, Rachel. Do you want to follow this perverse tribal
trail in a dreary neurotic search for reasons to beat yourself up,
or might you just exult in being alive?'

No one said anything.

'Have I made myself clear?' asked the baroness.

Rachel looked back at her and laughed. 'Abundantly clear,
Jack. It's good to have you back.'

Acknowledgements

I've been researching this for years and longing to write it, but other projects and life got in the way.

I owe many many thanks to a large number of friends and acquaintances who've variously visited art exhibitions with me, talked and laughed and expostulated with me about conceptual art, listened to my rants and given me helpful suggestions. I have to single out Colm de Barra, Lizzie Bawdon, Rob Bryant, Tony Cahill, Stephen Cang, Mary Devine, Emily Dyer, Barbara Sweetman FitzGerald, Elizabeth Gibbons, Dylan Haskins, Imogen Hartmann, Jo Henderson, Lucinda Hodge, David Martin Jones, Kathryn Kennison, John Lippitt, Jason McCue, James McGuire, Janet McIver, Sean O'Callaghan, Robert Salisbury, Alec Swanson, and David Stuart Taylor, but there were several others.

My beloved Carol Scott, who has been my minder for twenty one years, was as wonderful as ever. Jane Conway-Gordon (who has the misfortune to be my agent as well as close friend) performed the delicate calculation of knowing when to kick me and when to empathise. Nina Clarke, as ever, was the great encourager and made valuable comments on the manuscript, as did my brother Owen, generous, as always, with his time and his prodigious knowledge.

I feel real gratitude to those of my readers who kept nagging me to get writing fiction again, to my American agent,

Jane Chelius, and to all at Poisoned Pen for keeping the faith, particularly Barbara Peters, the Evil Editor revered by all, Rob Rosenwald, and Jessica Tribble.

I read many books and much journalism relating to the madder aspects of the art world. I owe most to Roger Kimball's *The Rape of the Masters* (which also provided the epigraph), Don Thompson's *The $12 Million Stuffed Shark: The Curious Economics of Contemporary Art and Auction Houses*, Sarah Thornton's *Seven Days in the Art World,* to the Stuckist website, and to the art criticism of Brian Sewell, who so often seemed to be the only sane person in the lunatic asylum that is the world of contemporary art.